MEET THE GIRL TALK CHARACTERS

Sabrina Wells is petite, with curly auburn hair, sparkling hazel eyes, and a bubbly personality. Sabrina loves magazines, shopping, sleepovers, and most of all, she loves talking to her best friends.

Katie Campbell is a straight-A student and super athlete. With her blond hair, blue eyes, and matching clothes, she's everyone's idea of Little Miss Perfect. But Katie has a few surprises for everyone, including herself!

Randy Zak has just moved to Acorn Falls from New York City, and is she ever cool! With her radical spiked haircut and her hip New York clothes, Randy teaches everyone just how much fun it is to be different.

Allison Cloud is a Native American Indian. Allison's supersmart and really beautiful. But she has one major problem: She's thirteen years old, five foot seven, and still growing!

Girl Talk

STEALING THE SHOW

By L. E. Blair

GIRL TALK® series created by Western Publishing Company, Inc.

Western Publishing Company, Inc., Racine, Wisconsin 53404

R MCMXCIII

Text by Crystal DiMeo

Chapter One

"Hi, Katie!" I said, greeting my best friend, Katie Campbell. "Ohmygosh! Where's my math book? Katie, have you seen my math book?" I dumped everything in my knapsack on the floor in front of the locker that Katie and I share. I searched frantically for my seventh-grade algebra book.

"Calm down, Sabs. It's right there," Katie said, laughing and pointing to the book I held in my left hand. "What's got you so excited?"

"Don't you know?" I answered. "Today is the day they announce which play the seventh-grade class will be doing this year. I can't wait to see what it is so I can pick which part I want to play. I hardly slept last night. I am so excited! I hope it's a comedy, or a musical — like *Annie*. That would be a great part for me with all this red hair."

I looked into the small mirror taped on the

inside of our locker door, and I tugged at one red curl. My hair is very long, curly, and thick. Most people call it red, but it's really auburn.

"Or maybe it will be a drama. *Romeo and Juliet* would be perfect, it's very romantic . . . ." I looked at Katie, who had this smile on her face.

"Sabs," said Katie, interrupting me, "let's walk past the music room on our way to our next class and see what's been posted about the play. That way you'll know exactly what the play is going to be, and you'll stop worrying."

Katie is always so calm and logical. That's probably why she's my best friend. I'm always getting a little excited about things.

"Okay," I said, slamming shut the locker door, completely ignoring my knapsack strap, which was hanging out of the bottom of the locker like a tail.

Katie, who's the neatest person I know, glanced down at the strap and sighed. As usual, she looked very pretty in a white sweatshirt with a pink miniskirt, pink anklets, and a pink ribbon in her long, straight blond hair. Her part of the locker is always perfectly neat, too. My books usually fall out whenever we open the door.

"I'll straighten up the locker later," I promised Katie. Then I grabbed her arm and half dragged her down the hallway toward the music room. "Come on, let's go!"

A sign-up sheet for auditions was hanging on the music room door, and a group of people was standing in front of it. Dr. Rossi, the drama and music teacher, was inside the classroom. Dr. Rossi isn't a medical doctor, but he has a degree in music, so he's called a "doctor." I think he spent almost eight years in college. To me, that's like being in school forever! I plan to be an actress when I grow up, and I'm sure glad that actresses don't have to spend years in college. Four years is definitely long enough for me.

I stood on my toes to see over everyone's heads. I'm only four foot ten and three-quarter inches tall, but I know I'll start getting taller soon. My mom says that I just have to have patience.

Finally enough people moved out of the way so that I could see what was on the sign-up sheet — *Grease: The Musical*.

"*Grease*! That's awesome!" I cried to Katie,

clutching her arm. "The lead role is Sandy, and she gets to fall in love with this gorgeous guy, Danny. It's so romantic! They even get to kiss in the last scene!"

"I know," said Katie. "I saw the movie with John Travolta and Olivia Newton-John. So, Sabrina, what part are you going to try out for?"

"Well, Sandy, of course," I said, surprised that she even had to ask. Naturally, I was going to try out for the lead role! If I really wanted to be a professional actress, I had to get as much experience on the stage as I could.

"Ha!" someone behind me said loudly. I spun around to see Stacy "the Great" Hansen standing there laughing at me. "I can't believe *you're* going to try out for the part of Sandy, Sabrina," Stacy taunted me. "I remember you in fifth-grade chorus — you can't sing a note! Besides, you don't look like Olivia Newton-John at all. She has long blond hair, like mine. The only actress you look like is that short red-headed little girl from the musical *Annie*!"

I just stood there, staring at her. I can never think of a good comeback line when it comes to Stacy the Great. I mean, okay, Stacy is right about her looking like Olivia Newton-John. But she doesn't have to talk about the way *I* look!

Stacy pushed past me to the audition sign-up sheet. She wrote her name in big letters in the column marked "Sandy."

Eva Malone, one of Stacy's best friends, stood nearby, laughing at what Stacy had just said to me. She took a pen, walked over to the sign-up sheet, and wrote her own name under "Rizzo," another character in the play. There was no way she could try out for the Sandy part because Stacy would have a fit. Rizzo is a pretty big part, too, though.

Ooh! Stacy makes me so mad! I usually don't have any problem making friends with people, but Stacy is different. Katie says that Stacy is jealous of me because I have so many friends, but I don't know if that's true. Anyway, when it comes to confrontations with Stacy, I just turn to mush!

"Well, we'll just wait and see!" I finally retorted and signed my name in capital letters right under Stacy's in the "Sandy" column. Then I grabbed Katie's arm and walked quickly down the hall. I could feel my body blush coming on. It always starts with my face turning red. Then it travels down until I'm bright red all over. It's so embarrassing!

"Sabs," Katie said when we had safely walked away from Stacy and Eva, "you know I'm your best friend, and I want you to be happy, but . . . " Katie hesitated. "Can you sing?"

Katie's question was half drowned out by the final warning bell for class. We had to run or we'd be late, so I didn't have a chance to give her an answer.

I can learn to sing, I thought to myself, as I ran to class. Actresses do it all the time. Besides, this was only the first step in my acting career. The lead part in a school production of *Grease* would send me on to high school plays and then Broadway! Playing the part of Sandy was just what I needed to launch my acting career.

Math class seemed to go on forever. When it was finally over, I got a chance to talk to Katie again when we met up at our locker before going on to band class, which we also have together.

"I'm going to go to the video store and rent *Grease* after school today. Do you want to come over?" I asked Katie.

"I think I can come over later. It sounds like fun."

"What sounds like fun?" Randy Zak asked, walking up to us. She looked down at me through a pair of cat's-eye sunglasses. I remember how much she surprised me when I ran into her on our first day at Bradley Junior High. She's from New York City and very cool, and different from anyone I have ever met before. She wears the wildest clothes, and she's into music and art. As a matter of fact, her mother's an artist. It's great that she's become one of my best friends.

"We're going to rent *Grease* and watch it over at my house after school. Do you want to come?" I asked Randy.

"Hi, guys. What's going on?" Allison Cloud said, walking up and standing next to Randy. She's another of my best friends. Al's a Native American, and she's gorgeous. She has long, shiny black hair that hangs down to her waist and great big sparkling brown eyes. Plus, she's very tall and was even offered the chance to become a professional model in New York City.

"Sabs wants to rent *Grease* after school today," Randy explained. She made a face when she said the name of the movie, then bent to retie the laces of her ankle-high black steel-toed boots. It figured that *Grease* wouldn't be Randy's kind of movie. She's really into horror films.

"I'll have to call home and make sure I don't have to watch Charlie first," Allison told us. She has to baby-sit for her seven-year-old brother a lot. He's very cute, but he's always getting into trouble. But that's what brothers are like. I should know — I have four of them.

"Well, call during your study hall. It'll be a lot of fun. We can make microwave popcorn," I said persuasively, looking up at her. Allison is almost a foot taller than me.

"Okay," Allison promised. Al is the kind of person who loves study hall because it gives her time to read. Right now she's reading a book called *The Lord of the Rings*, and she's constantly reading us her favorite parts. Al is so smart that I swear she reads a book a day. Sometimes she even reads the same book twice! And they're not easy books, either. Al has already read books that my older brother Luke has to read for his high school classes!

"Are you guys going to try out for the

play?" I asked. "It would be great if we could all be in it together."

"I can't, Sabs. I have to keep up with my schoolwork," Katie apologized. I just gave her a look. I could see that I was going to have my work cut out for me trying to convince her that she could be in the play and keep up with her homework, too. She'd have a great time, I was sure of that.

"Well, how about you two? Come on, it'll be uh . . . uh, rewarding!" I said, looking from Al to Randy.

"*Rewarding*?" said Randy with bewilderment. Then we all looked at one another and burst out laughing.

Allison just shook her head. Al's kind of shy. Being onstage would be really good for her, I think. I read an article in one of my teen magazines that said the best way to get over a fear is to face it. I guess everyone's different. All I know is that being on the stage is for me.

"No way will you get me onstage for some school play," Randy announced firmly.

"What's wrong with school plays?" I asked, staring at her.

"Nothing, Sabs," Randy replied. "*Grease* is

just not my thing. Now, if it was a horror movie like *Rabid Grannies*, that would be completely different."

"*Rabid Grannies*?" Katie asked, raising her eyebrows. "What's that about?"

"It's awesome. There are these two old grandmothers who live together in this big old house, and their families are trying to get their money. Anyway, the grannies have a birthday party, and after they drink this wine, they get rabid. They start frothing at the mouth, and their fingernails grow really long and they grow hair all over their bodies."

"Gross!" I exclaimed.

"And then they start eating their relatives," Randy continued gleefully.

"Stop! I'm going to be sick," Katie moaned.

"Back to the play," Allison cut in. "Maybe we could work backstage on lights or scenery or something," she suggested.

"Hey! Working on the lighting would be cool," Randy replied.

"You know, I could probably help out sometimes, too," Katie added.

"Great! This is going to be absolutely incredible, you'll see." I couldn't wait for school to end so that I could get the *Grease* video and start learning my part for tomorrow's audition.

I said good-bye to Randy and Allison, and Katie and I walked to band class together.

When I walked into the classroom, I grabbed a music stand from the closet and sat down in the clarinet section.

I took out the mouthpiece from my clarinet case and started to suck on the reed. That's the only part I don't really like about playing the clarinet — besides practicing. I always feel so silly sitting there with this piece of wood sticking out of my mouth. The worst part is that I can't even talk to anyone while I'm doing it.

Mr. Metcalf, the band leader, came in and told us all to take out the new jazz song that he'd given us last week and to start warming up. I leaned over to pull the music out of my case. At the same time, I noticed a pair of white high-top sneakers stop right beside my chair.

I looked up, the reed still sticking out of my mouth like a big tongue, and there stood Cameron Booth.

He smiled at me and sat down in the seat next to mine. I felt my face getting hot and then the tips of my ears. And then my back. My body blush was coming on again. Meanwhile, I couldn't take my eyes off Cameron. He's the cutest guy in the class, and I've had a crush on him forever — at least two weeks. He has blond hair and blue eyes and the greatest dimples when he smiles.

"Hey, Sabs. Are you trying out for the play?" Cameron asked me as he took his oboe out of its case.

I started to open my mouth, but luckily I remembered the reed. I quickly took it out of my mouth and blushed even harder. How embarrassing!

"Yes," I said quickly, hoping that he hadn't noticed. "I just signed up. Are you trying out, too?"

"I sure am! I just signed up for the part of Danny. I don't know if I'll get it or not, though. There are a lot of really good singers trying out," Cameron told me.

Well, if I was in charge, I would pick Cameron Booth for sure! I pictured Cameron and me together onstage as Danny and Sandy, holding hands and singing to each other. I felt my face start to get even hotter. I shoved the reed back into my mouth and pretended to be studying the music on the stand in front of me.

I could barely sit still for the rest of class. I was just dying to tell Katie about Cameron. Wow! I just love acting! Danny and Sandy . . . Sabrina and Cameron . . . It was meant to be!

Chapter Two

Finally the bell rang at the end of science, my last class of the day. I ran to my locker to meet Al, Katie, and Randy and practically dragged them out of school and down the street toward the video store. Luckily, Acorn Falls is so small that we can walk to almost everything, like school and the shops on Main Street, which is where Main Street Video is.

"Hey, Sabs! What's the rush?" Randy called to me. She slowed down her pace and was about ten feet behind me when I turned around. I was almost at the door of the video store. I couldn't wait to see if the *Grease* tape was there.

"Come on, guys! I don't want anyone else to get the movie before us." Just as I said that, Stacy and her clones came around the corner behind us.

"Oh, no! Hurry up," I yelled, frantically

pulling Katie, Randy, and Allison into the store. "We've got to find the tape and rent it before she does!" I said, pointing out the window.

Randy, Al, and Katie looked outside and saw Stacy, Eva, and B.Z. coming down the street toward Main Street Video. We all turned around and started to look through the racks.

"There must be thousands of tapes in here," Katie moaned, looking helplessly around at the walls lined with tapes.

"How are we ever going to find it?" I wailed.

"Look," Allison said, pointing. "Everything is separated into categories." Trust Al to notice something like that! I'll bet she's the only kid at Bradley who actually understands the Dewey Decimal System in the library. "These are the new releases," she continued, walking over to the wall on our right. "And those are the horror movies."

"Awesome!" Randy called, walking to the section Allison had shown us. "Let's get one of these, too. Look! *I Spit on Your Grave!*"

"We don't have time!" I told her. "We have to find *Grease.*" I turned around just in time to see Stacy and her friends walking in the door.

I whirled back around to face the walls and walls of tapes surrounding us, and started searching the shelves. Stacy and her clones were in the store looking for my movie! I had to find it first! The question was, was it a drama or a comedy?

"Uh-oh!" I suddenly heard Allison exclaim. I walked down to the shelf where she was standing to see what was wrong. It didn't take me long to figure it out.

Stacy Hansen, a smug grin on her face, was walking toward us from the back wall. In her right hand she held the *Grease* videotape jacket.

"Of course! It was under musicals," Allison whispered, shaking her head. "Why didn't we think of that?"

"Why, Sabrina Wells! I didn't know you were here," Stacy crowed loudly with a fake laugh. She held up the tape case. "Doesn't Olivia Newton-John have the nicest long blond hair?" Stacy asked, flipping her own long blond hair over one shoulder.

"I can't wait to see this movie," Eva Malone gushed, standing next to Stacy. She smiled, and the metal of her braces flashed brightly. Those braces are the reason that my brother Sam and his friends nicknamed Eva "Jaws." "We'll do so much better at the auditions once we've seen the movie, too," she gloated.

B. Z. Latimer, another of Stacy's followers, smirked at us from beside Eva.

"Too bad there's only one copy, Sabrina," Stacy went on. "Good luck tomorrow!" She and her friends turned away, laughing.

I was so angry, I could almost feel the steam pouring out of my ears! I could tell that my face was red because it felt so hot. That Stacy! She had ruined my chances of getting ready for the audition!

"Sabs! Allison! Over here!" Katie called to us. She was standing by the checkout counter. Behind the counter was Peter, the goalie from Bradley's ice hockey team. His father owns the video store, and he works there sometimes after school.

Then I noticed a white plastic bag hanging from Katie's arm. A white plastic bag with a tape in it! Why had she rented a movie? Stacy had already found the *Grease* tape, and I wasn't in the mood to watch anything else. I started to ask her about it, but before I could do more than open my mouth, Randy began pushing me toward the door.

"I got it!" Katie whispered loudly as we rushed out the video store, a huge smile on her face. "Let's go before Stacy freaks out."

"But . . . but . . . how did you get it?" I asked, totally confused. "Stacy had it in her hand. I saw it!"

"That wasn't the tape, Sabs! That was only the cover. You have to bring the cover up to the counter, and then they get the tape out of the back room for you," Randy explained.

"Haven't you ever rented a tape before?" Allison asked, sounding surprised.

"Yeah, but usually Sam goes to the counter because I'm too busy trying to make up my mind," I told her.

"I can believe that!" Randy said with a laugh.

"Well, anyway," said Katie. "I explained everything to Peter. He went into the back room and got the tape for me right away. Poor Peter. I'll bet Stacy is yelling at him right now," Katie said.

For a second, I felt sorry for Peter. Then I thought about how mad Stacy probably was, and started to laugh.

"Hello! I'm home," I yelled as loudly as I could when we walked into my house. Mom got all of us into the habit of doing that because she needs all the help she can get to keep track of five kids.

"I'll be down in a minute!" I heard my mother call back from upstairs.

"We're going to use the VCR for a while. Okay? Thanks," I hollered. I ran into the family room without waiting for an answer.

I popped the tape into the VCR, turned on the TV, pressed PLAY, and plopped down on the floor to watch, dragging a pillow off the coach to lean on. Katie and Allison sat on the couch, and Randy sat Indian-style in my father's favorite chair. We waited and waited for the fuzz to clear up and the movie to start, but all we got was more fuzz.

"Oh, no! What's wrong?" I cried. How could this happen? I absolutely had to see this tape, and it was broken!

"Sabrina, what's the matter?" my mother asked, coming into the room.

"There's something wrong with the tape or the machine or something," I cried. "What am I going to do now?"

My mother walked over to the machine, pulled out the tape, and started laughing. "There's nothing wrong with anything," she said, shaking her head. "This tape needs to be rewound, that's all." She put the tape back in and pressed the REWIND button, still smiling.

Katie, Al, and Randy all started to giggle. I tried to ignore them, but pretty soon I had to start laughing, too. It was pretty funny, after all.

"Sabs, you are so . . ." Katie searched for the right word, still gasping with laughter.

"Dramatic!" Allison filled in. They were right, of course. But actresses are supposed to be dramatic. "What's so important about this tape, anyway?" my mother asked, handing me the remote control.

"It's *Grease*, Mom. That's the play this year, and I'm trying out for the lead tomorrow," I explained.

My mom is the only person in our family who doesn't think that my dream of becoming an actress is a silly phase that I'll grow out of. Since I'm the youngest of five kids, everybody is always telling me that I'll "grow out of it." When I say I want to be an actress when I grow up, I'm just as serious as Luke, who is already filling out applications for college and picking out majors and stuff. Thank goodness Mom always listens to me. Maybe it's because I'm her only girl.

"Okay. Your tape is all ready," Mom announced. She pushed the PLAY button on the VCR and walked out of the family room toward the kitchen.

"Oh, wait!" I called, jumping up and running to the telephone table to grab a pencil and some paper. "I have to take notes." All good actresses take notes on the roles they're going to play.

"Take notes?" Randy asked. "It's not like this is *Gone With the Wind* or anything, Sabs."

"Sabrina, I'm going out for a minute," Mom called from the hall.

"Good-bye," we all yelled back.

The movie came on and we heard the sounds of "Love Is a Many-Splendored Thing." Waves crashed on the beach, and Danny and Sandy were walking hand in hand across the screen.

"How corny!" Randy groaned.

"Shh! I think it's romantic," I whispered.

I started writing frantically, trying to get

down every line that Sandy said. That was pretty hard, since she says more than almost anybody else in the movie!

"Ugh! What is this?" Sam exclaimed as he walked in, grabbing his throat and pretending to choke. "*Grease*! What a sappy movie!"

"Shut up, Sam. I'm trying to listen!" I told him.

Sam is my twin brother and was born four whole minutes before me. He never lets me forget it, either. Sometimes it's really great having a twin — I mean, we can practically read each other's minds. But other times it can be a real pain, especially since we have a lot of the same friends. Everybody says we look exactly alike, but I don't think it's true. Sam does have red hair and freckles like I do, but everything else about us is completely different.

Sam disappeared into the kitchen and came out again with a yellow dish towel hanging over his head as if it were a blond wig. He sang one of the songs from the movie in a high, squeaky voice and then started dancing around the room.

Katie picked up a small blue pillow from the couch and threw it at him.

"Hey, Sam. You're pretty good. Maybe you should try out for the play," Randy teased. "You'd look great in a poodle skirt and a blond wig!"

We all laughed and started throwing pillows at Sam until he ran out of the room.

"Ooh, this is a good part," I said, picking up my pad and starting to write as fast as I could again. I felt as if my hand was going to fall off. "Oh, no, wait! I missed a line!" I cried and grabbed the remote control to rewind the movie.

"Sabs, if you keep pushing REWIND and PAUSE, we'll never finish watching the movie!" Katie cried. She got up and went out to the kitchen. "Can I get something to eat?" she asked. Katie knows where everything is in my house. She's here so often that she's almost a member of the family.

"Sure, " I yelled, still writing. "You know where everything is."

Just then Mom walked back into the room. "Hi, girls. Sabrina, I got you a present, but you seem very busy." Mom had a big grin on her face.

I hate it when she teases me like that. I

stopped the tape and jumped up off the couch.

"Come on, Mom! Please?" I begged, jumping up and down in front of her. I love getting presents — especially when they're a surprise.

"Well, all right." Mom gave in. She pulled a brown paper bag out from behind her back.

I ripped open the bag, and inside was a recording of the *Grease* sound track!

"Thank you!" I cried. Now I could practice my singing until it was perfect! I wondered if there were going to be any talent scouts in the audience. One of them might even love my acting and sign me up for a Broadway play!

Just then Katie came back from the kitchen with a huge bowl of microwave popcorn. I suddenly realized that I was practically starving. I love popcorn. It also happens to be low in calories. Cameras always make you look ten pounds heavier than you really are, so popcorn is the perfect food for a soon-to-be-famous actress!

Chapter Three

The only turntable we have in our house, besides my parents' good one, is in Sam and Mark's room. I decided to practice my singing in there. As soon as Allison, Randy, and Katie went home for dinner, I ran upstairs and knocked on the door to my brothers' room.

I heard Sam grunt as I opened the door.

"I have to listen to this record," I said as I ran over to the stereo.

"No way!" Sam screamed over the noise of the Nintendo game he was playing. He didn't even look up.

"You know Mom says you're supposed to let me use the stereo if you're not using it yourself." I put one hand on the doorknob as if I was going downstairs to get Mom.

"Oh, okay," Sam said, grumbling, and he turned up the sound on his computer.

I put on the first song and I wrote down all

the words and who sang them. Then I played it again and started to sing Sandy's first part. I didn't think I sounded that bad. In fact, I thought I sounded just as good as the actors in the movie. I looked over and saw Sam holding his ears. He's always teasing me. I was not about to let him bother me, though.

"Where is that horrible singing coming from?" Mark yelled over the record and the video game as he walked into the room.

Mark, who's thirteen and my next older brother after Sam, teases me all the time, too. Mark has lighter hair than Sam and I do, and he's taller. Mark proves that there's a good chance that I'll get taller. He didn't really begin to grow until this year, when he started eighth grade.

"Oh, sorry, Sabs," Mark apologized, pretending that he hadn't known that it was me singing. "Why are you singing in here?" Mark asked.

"She's practicing for *Grease*, the school play," Sam answered without looking up from his computer.

"I'm not that bad, am I, Mark?" I asked, hoping he would be serious for a minute.

"Well, you're no teen recording star," he replied.

I put both hands on my hips and stared at him for a second, trying to decide if that was some kind of backward compliment.

"What role are you trying out for, anyway?" he asked.

"Sandy," I told him.

Sam burst out laughing. Before I knew it, Mark was laughing, too.

I picked my notebook up from the floor, took my album off the stereo, and stomped out of the room. What did they know, anyway? They were just two dumb guys. What had Frenchy said in the movie? It was something about guys being fleas on rats. I smiled. I was already beginning to know the play.

I decided to practice my singing when Sam and Mark weren't around. I stayed in my room until dinner and studied the lines I had written down during the movie. One of the good things about being the only girl in the family is that I have my own bedroom.

Just after dinner, I went into the part of the attic where Mom keeps all of our old toys and clothes and stuff. I knew that there was a long blond wig in there somewhere from Halloween years ago when I had dressed up as a princess. I had decided to wear it for the audition. I mean, I didn't really need to wear it. So what if I didn't have real long blond hair like Stacy the Great and Olivia Newton-John? I'm still a good actress. But it wouldn't hurt to look the part. I stuffed the wig into my knapsack. I was just about to close the trunk when I saw a black skirt with a great fluffy pink poodle on it, and a cute white sweater with little buttons up the front. It was just about the right size, except that the skirt would probably have to be shortened a little bit. Underneath that was a sheer pink scarf. *What a great costume this would make*, I thought to myself.

Next I found a pair of black-and-white saddle shoes. They must have been my mom's when she was a teenager. I took off my sneakers and stuck my feet into them. They were a bit too big, but I was pretty sure they would be all right if I stuffed some paper in the toes and laced them up tightly. It was weird to think that my mother had actually worn clothes like these to school every day!

I suddenly heard the phone ringing and my

mother yelling that it was for me. I ran down the stairs as fast as I could to get it.

I grabbed the phone. "Hello, this is Sabrina."

"Hi, Sabs. It's Katie," I heard Katie's cheerful voice say on the other end of the line.

"Hi, Katie. What's up?" I replied, plopping down on the stairs.

"I just thought I would call and see how your practicing was going," Katie said. I could hear Katie's sister Emily's stereo playing loudly in the background.

"Well, I think it's going well," I told her. "I've learned a lot of the lines already."

"Are you nervous about the audition tomorrow?" Katie asked.

"Nervous? Of course not!" I said, trying to sound more confident than I really felt.

"Sabs?" said Katie doubtfully.

"Okay. Maybe just a little," I admitted. Katie knows me too well to be fooled.

"Well, Randy, Allison, and I are going to be there cheering for you," Katie told me. That made me feel a little better.

"Thanks," I said. "You guys are great."

"Oh! I just remembered," Katie went on.

"Emily said that when she was in her high school version of the play, she had to learn to do the hand jive and the Lindy and all those other weird dances they did in the movie."

"But I don't know how to do any of those things!" I moaned. I started to feel panicky. I thought I would be prepared if I knew all the songs and the lines. Now I had to learn dances, too?

"Don't worry about it. I'm sure they'll teach you during rehearsals," Katie said, trying to calm me down.

"But I wanted to have a head start on everybody!" I explained to her.

"Why don't you ask your parents," Katie suggested. "Didn't they grow up then?"

"Katie! That's an awesome idea! I'll go ask them right now."

"Good luck! I'll see you tomorrow. I'll meet you by our locker before first period," Katie said.

"Okay. Thanks, Katie," I said.

We said good-bye, and I hung up the phone and ran into the family room. "Mom! Dad!" I said, facing them as they sat on the couch. "Can you teach me how to do the hand Lindy, or the jive?"

Dad started to laugh and Mom giggled.

"I think you mean the hand jive and the Lindy," Mom said, smiling.

"Why on Earth do you want to learn those old dances?" my father asked.

"My school is putting on the play *Grease*, and I'm trying out for the lead," I explained to him quickly. "I want to have a head start on everyone at the auditions. So, can you teach me?"

"Well, Sabrina, I was born in the fifties and didn't really go out dancing until the sixties," Mom told me apologetically.

"Oh, please," I begged. "Don't you remember any of the dances?"

Finally my mother and father agreed to show me what they knew of the dances. They even dug out a bunch of old records. They looked great together, dancing all around the room. Somewhere in the middle of it all, Mark and Sam came running downstairs to find out what the noise was about. They took one look, shook their heads, and went right back upstairs again.

I kept watching and finally caught on to a

few of the steps. It was a lot of fun! By the time I got to bed, I was totally exhausted. I fell asleep right away, too tired even to think about the auditions.

Then I had the strangest dream. I dreamed that I was on television performing *Romeo and Juliet* when I suddenly stopped and began to dance the Lindy right in the middle of the show!

Chapter Four

After school I ran to my locker to drop off my books and pick up my knapsack. Randy and Allison were standing there waiting for me, and Katie had put up a surprise GOOD LUCK, SABRINA! sign on our locker.

We all walked to the auditorium together. Dr. Rossi passed out copies of the scene we were supposed to read. As soon as I got my copy, I sat down and started to rehearse it. I tried to memorize most of it, so I would seem as natural as possible.

I looked around and noticed that Stacy wasn't there yet. Could this mean that she'd decided not to try out? Somehow I doubted that.

The auditorium became more and more crowded with kids. I still didn't see Stacy anywhere, though. Dr. Rossi was just about to start when Stacy walked in.

"Real nice of her to show up before it started," Randy whispered.

"Look. She's fixing her hair!" I pointed out. "And she looks really calm."

"Don't worry. You'll do great," Allison assured me. "Just because Stacy looks good doesn't mean she can act."

"I hope you're right," I said. But then I saw Mr. Hansen sit down next to Dr. Rossi. Mr. Hansen is not only the principal of our school, but also Stacy's father.

"What is he doing here?" I whispered. "What if Mr. Hansen makes Dr. Rossi pick Stacy?"

"I don't think Mr. Hansen would do that," Katie said quickly.

"Sabrina Wells," Dr. Rossi called suddenly. I had been so lost in my thoughts that hearing my name made me jump. I got up, grabbed my knapsack with the wig in it, crawled over Katie so I could get to the aisle, and then walked up to the stage.

"All right, Sabrina. You'll be reading the part of Frenchy for this scene," Dr. Rossi told me with a kind smile.

"But I signed up for Sandy," I said weakly,

holding up my knapsack, as if that would make him understand.

"I know, Sabrina. But we're going to read different parts today. The part you read won't affect the part you get," Dr. Rossi explained to me. "We're just testing your acting ability." He smiled at me again. "Stacy Hansen," Dr. Rossi turned away from me and called out.

Stacy fixed her hair one last time and walked slowly onto the stage.

"Stacy, you'll be reading the part of Sandy in this scene," Dr. Rossi informed her.

Stacy smiled her totally phony thousand-watt smile at him and then turned around and smirked at me. I wanted to scream! I wanted to be Sandy!

"Charlotte Benson. Could you please read the part of Rizzo? Theresa Parker, you can read Patty Simcock's role. And Karen Eckert, you'll be reading Marty's part," Dr. Rossi directed. Then he walked off the stage to sit down.

"Okay, girls, go ahead and start the scene," Dr. Rossi called from the front row of seats. The first line was mine. I quickly cleared my throat and read it from the script.

I spoke in a squeaky voice and pretended to

chew gum, just like I remembered Frenchy had in the movie. I even remembered to project my voice toward the audience, the way the woman said to do on this "Learn to Act at Home" show I once saw on cable. Maybe if I did a good job playing Frenchy, Dr. Rossi would let me read Sandy's part next.

Stacy had the next line in the scene, but she hadn't been paying attention and didn't know where we were in the script. That must have made her nervous because she read the line as if we were in English class instead of onstage. Now Dr. Rossi would absolutely have to let me read for Sandy.

We read through the whole scene until we came to the part where the song was supposed to start. Charlotte, Theresa, and Karen did pretty well, but Stacy just kept on reading in this really flat voice. She said everything perfectly, but without any emotion.

When we were finished, Dr. Rossi asked us to return to our seats in the audience. Then it was the guys' turn to read. First he called Cameron Booth to read for Danny. Then he called the next person to read for Sonny: Sam Wells. Sam Wells? My brother, Sam? I hadn't even seen him sitting in the corner of the auditorium. What was he doing here? He was the one who had laughed at me and told me it was a dumb play. Boy, would I let him have it for making fun of me when he was planning to try out, too!

Then Dr. Rossi called Nick Robbins and Jason McKee to read for the parts of Doody and Kenicke, two more of the T-Birds, Danny's gang.

I listened as Sam read his first line. I had to admit that he sounded pretty good. But why shouldn't he? I'm sure that acting probably runs in our family.

Cameron read his part and he was great. He had combed his hair back the way Danny does in the play, and he was a terrific actor. He put himself right into the part. *Wow!* I thought to myself. *It would be awesome if we both got the leads.*

I thought that I'd done really well. But then it came time to sing. Dr. Rossi told us that we would each have a chance to sing the lead part in "Summer Nights." Almost everybody knew the tune, but a couple of people weren't too sure about the words. I was glad that Mom had gotten me that album!

Stacy was the first girl to sing. I was starting to get a funny feeling in my throat, like it was closing up. I felt as if I couldn't even talk. I probably just needed to rest my voice after working so hard to project my words to the back of the auditorium.

Dr. Rossi started playing the piano and Stacy opened her mouth. She was great! Suddenly I wished I'd never even heard about this stupid play. Why had I even bothered to try out? Stacy had been taking singing, dancing, and piano lessons ever since she was four! How could I compete with that? Then I remembered how badly Stacy had done at the reading. So maybe I couldn't sing quite as well as Stacy Hansen. But I was still a much better actress. I had to get this part!

When Stacy finished, Dr. Rossi stopped playing. "That's fine, Stacy. Thank you. Sabrina Wells, please come to the stage and sing the lead for the girls."

I took a deep breath, grabbed my knapsack and walked toward the steps that led backstage. I had to go behind the stage in order to come out in front.

As fast as I could, I opened up my knapsack and grabbed the wig and the clothes. I quickly slipped on the skirt, sweater, and shoes. I tied the scarf around my neck and ran out onstage. No one made a sound. Everyone onstage and in the audience just looked at me. Then Dr. Rossi cleared his throat. "Um, are you ready now, Sabrina?"

Suddenly I heard a noise behind me. I turned around and saw Katie, Randy, and Allison. They were all waving and smiling. They looked a little nervous, too, because they shouldn't have been backstage. But it was just what I needed to calm down. I have the absolute best friends in the world.

I turned back around quickly and nodded at Dr. Rossi. Then I heard the music start.

I started too high and kind of squeaked at the last note. I stopped dead. Had that sound actually come from me?

I started the next line too low. I heard someone giggling behind me. I turned. It was Stacy! She poked Eva, who snorted and whispered back. I turned away and tried to concentrate on singing better.

"'Summer days, drifted away to, oooh,

those summer nights,'" I finished on an especially low note. I knew I had sounded just awful. All I wanted to do was run off the stage and hide. I pulled off the wig and hid it behind my back. I felt my body blush starting. How could I have done so badly in front of my friends, and Stacy — and especially Cameron!

Dr. Rossi stopped playing and thanked me. He asked me to return to my seat and then called the next girl up to sing. I ran backstage. I was practically in tears as I took off the wig, skirt, and shoes and stuffed them back in my knapsack.

On the way back to my seat, Sam whispered to me. "I think you were a little off-key," he pointed out.

"Only a little?" I asked hopefully. I guess the recording is different from hearing it live. Then I realized I was talking to Sam. "Hey, I thought you said it was a sappy movie."

"I said it was a sappy movie. The play will be great if my friends and I are in it!" he told me. He walked to the opposite side of the auditorium to sit down.

"I guess my singing didn't improve too much from all that practice," I mumbled to my friends when I sat down next to them again. They had all managed to get back in their seats without being caught backstage. I was really embarrassed. I looked from Al to Katie to Randy. "Can we go now?" I said, grabbing my knapsack and zipping it closed so that I didn't have to look at that blond wig or those clothes anymore. My friends followed me up the aisle and out of the auditorium.

"Don't be silly. You did fine," Katie assured me as we walked down the empty hallway.

Katie is a great friend, but a terrible liar. "Thanks," I said anyway.

"Really, Sabs. You did an awesome job with the lines," Randy said. "You sounded just like Frenchy did in the movie." It felt good to hear Randy say that. She is always honest. If she said that I was awesome, then I must have been at least okay.

I started to feel a little better. Maybe I still had a chance.

"Thanks, Ran. But I wish I could have read Sandy's part," I said. "I'm going back into that auditorium to tell Dr. Rossi that I want to read the lines for Sandy!"

"I'm sure that Dr. Rossi can tell how well

you can act by any part that you read," Allison said quickly.

"Yeah, Sabs. That's true," Katie agreed.

"Well, he could definitely see that Stacy isn't into it," Randy added.

"I guess so. I guess there's nothing more for me to do," I replied with a sigh. "Dr. Rossi said that he would put the cast list up on his office door Monday morning," I told them as we walked out the front door of the school.

"Wow! You have to wait the whole weekend?" Katie asked sympathetically.

I nodded.

"Try not to think about it," Allison suggested.

"I know. It's just so hard!" I told her.

"Hey! Let's go to Fitzie's for a sundae or something?" Randy asked. "I could really use some food."

My friends know exactly how to cheer me up. Allison and Katie both agreed. As for me, I figured that a chocolate-chip cookie sundae might be just what I needed to feel a whole lot better.

Chapter Five

We got to Fitzie's and sat in a corner booth. From there, we could see the whole place and everybody in it. There were a lot of kids from Bradley hanging out, as usual, but I didn't see anyone from the auditions. I have to say I was relieved.

We all ordered. Randy got a soda and some french fries. Katie and Al each got a double malted. I got my chocolate-chip cookie sundae. When our order came, Randy started talking about how one of the major things missing in Acorn Falls is a good deli.

"We have a deli," I said, confused. "Deli Delicious. They sell cold cuts and stuff," I told her, digging into the whipped cream on my sundae.

"You've obviously never been to a New York deli. One day I'm going to take all of you guys to New York for a visit, and then you'll see," Randy promised. "I'll introduce all of you to my dad, too."

Randy's father produces music videos and commercials in New York City. Just thinking about meeting him makes my stomach do flip-flops.

"That would be fun," I said through a mouthful of ice cream. "We could go to Broadway, and maybe I'll get discovered." I started getting excited. After all, Broadway is where all the big stars and producers hang out.

"I'd love to go see where you used to live in New York," Allison agreed.

I was just starting to relax and enjoy my ice cream when about twenty people walked into Fitzie's. It seemed like everyone from the auditions had gotten there all at once.

Cameron and Stacy walked past our table. Cameron smiled at me and said "hi". I was so embarrassed that he had seen my audition that when I opened my mouth, nothing came out.

"What's the matter, Sabrina?" Stacy asked nastily. "Got a frog in your throat? It sure sounded like it at the audition!" Some of the other girls who had been at the audition laughed with her. I wanted to crawl under the table. At least Cameron didn't laugh. He just walked over to another booth nearby and sat down. Stacy, of course, sat next to him. It figured. Lately, as soon as I get a crush on someone, Stacy's after him, too.

Even over the noise of the rest of the Fitzie's crowd, I could still hear Stacy giggling and flirting with Cameron. She was acting as if they were already Danny and Sandy!

Cameron and Stacy would look really good together as a couple with their matching blond hair. I could just see them standing in the spotlight, looking into each other's eyes and singing . . . .

"Oooh! I wish I had blond hair!" I blurted out, tugging hard at a red curl that had gotten loose from my braid.

"What?" Al, Katie, and Randy all looked at me in surprise. I guess that I must have sounded strange, making that comment about my hair out of the blue like that.

"Oh, nothing," I said. Maybe the wig hadn't been enough. If I really looked the part, then maybe Dr. Rossi would choose me, even though my singing wasn't so good. Suddenly this great idea came to me. I knew exactly what to do to get the part.

I could hardly wait. I didn't even finish my sundae. I told Katie, Allison, and Randy that I had to get home. Katie asked me if everything was okay, and I told her it was, but that I had just remembered that I had something really important to do.

I ran around the corner to the drugstore and started going up and down the aisles. What I needed for my great idea had to be here somewhere. Finally I found what I was looking for — the hair dye section. I could have blond hair as nice as Stacy's! All I had to do was figure out which kind of dye to use. It would have to be the type of dye that wouldn't last forever and would work on auburn hair. But there were so many different brands on the shelves. Which one did I want?

I must have looked really confused because pretty soon a saleslady came over to ask if I needed any help.

"I want to dye my hair blond," I explained. "But I only want it to last for about a month."

"Well, you can try this. This is a temporary hair-coloring product. It washes out after ten washes," she told me, holding up one of the boxes. "Or this one might do. Except that it's a longer-lasting treatment."

I decided to buy the first one. If I needed to, I could just keep dying my hair until the play was over.

"I don't know why you would want to change the color of your hair, though," the saleslady went on. "It's such a beautiful shade of red."

"Thank you," I said. "I'll take this one." The box I picked had a picture of a beautiful woman with blond hair.

When I got home, I found a note saying that my parents had gone out for an early dinner with some friends. Mom had left dinner for us in the refrigerator, and all we had to do was pop it into the microwave. A "P.S." at the bottom of the note was from Mark, Sam, and Luke. They were playing basketball and then having dinner at a friend's house nearby. My oldest brother, Matthew, is away at college, so I didn't have to worry about him.

Great! Now I had the whole house to myself and the whole evening to do my hair and surprise my parents.

I ran up to my room, changed into an old T-shirt and sweatpants, grabbed a towel, and went straight to the bathroom to get started on my transformation.

I read the directions quickly. "For gray hair." No, that wasn't me. "For dark brown or red hair, leave solution on for fifteen minutes, then wash out."

That sounded easy enough. I put on the clear plastic gloves that came in the box. I felt like a surgeon or something, except that the gloves were big and slippery, so it was kind of hard to hold on to stuff.

I shook the bottle of dye until my arms ached and then opened it. It smelled horrible. I hoped it didn't make my hair smell like that! I squirted the dye all over my head and rubbed it in really good, just like the directions said. I looked down and noticed that I had dribbled dye all over the bathroom floor. I'd have to remember to clean it up before Mom got home.

I put the plastic bag over my head and sat there in the bathroom for fifteen minutes. It seemed as if the clock wasn't moving at all, but finally it was time to wash out my hair.

I dunked my head in the sink and then rubbed my hair with a towel. *When I look in the mirror, I'll be a blond,* I kept thinking to myself. *Then I'll look just like Sandy. Cameron and I will make the perfect couple!* I took off the towel and looked in the mirror.

"Oh, no!" I screamed. Looking back at me from the mirror was a girl with bright orange curly hair!

"How did this happen? I did everything exactly the way the package said!" I exclaimed. I grabbed the box off the counter and read it again. Then I noticed the color chart on the side, which said, "If your natural color is this, it will become this."

I found dark red on the chart. Next to it was written, "Lighter red to strawberry blond." Strawberry blond! Yuk! I looked like a Sunkist orange! Why hadn't I finished reading all of the instructions?

I looked down at my watch. I didn't have much time before my parents or my brothers came home, and I just couldn't let them see me like this. What about school? I couldn't hide this!

Maybe if I washed my hair ten times, the dye would wash out. I dunked my head back under the sink and scrubbed and scrubbed.

Each time I peeked at the mirror, I could see that my hair was still the same awful orange color. I was running out of time — and shampoo! My fingers were like prunes and my scalp hurt. I just wanted to cry.

I wrapped my head in a towel so that none of my brothers would see me if they came home. They would never let me live this down! I had to call Katie.

Chapter Six

EMILY: Hello! Emily Campbell speaking.

SABRINA: Hi, Emily. This is Sabrina. Is Katie there? I've got to talk to her right away!

EMILY: Just a minute. (*Calling*) Katie! Telephone!

KATIE: Hello?

SABRINA: Katie! It's me. You've got to help me!

KATIE: Sabs, what's wrong?

SABRINA: Oh, Katie! I tried to make myself blond for the play and now my hair's orange!

KATIE: You did what?

SABRINA: I dyed my hair! I thought if I was blond like Stacy, Dr. Rossi would give me the lead, even though I can't sing as well as she does. But it didn't work that way!

KATIE: Your hair's orange?

SABRINA: Yes! I tried washing it out, but it didn't help. What am I going to do?

KATIE: Don't worry about it. We'll think of something. You stay there, and I'll call Randy and Allison. Maybe they'll know what to do. We'll be over as soon as we can.

SABRINA: Hurry!

KATIE: We will!

(Katie calls Allison.)

ALLISON: Hello? Allison Cloud speaking.

KATIE: Al, it's Katie. Listen, there's an emergency.

ALLISON: What's wrong? Is someone hurt?

KATIE: No, it's nothing like that. Remember how upset Sabrina was about her audition today?

ALLISON: Yes. She even left Fitzie's early.

KATIE: Right. Well, she left early so that she could go home and dye her hair blond! She thought it would give her a better chance of getting the part she wanted.

ALLISON: Oh, no! Let me guess. Something went wrong with the hair dye, right?

KATIE: Al, Sabs has orange hair! We have to help her!

ALLISON: Orange hair! Quick! Call Randy. She'll know what to do. I'm going to go straight over to Sabs's house and calm her down.

KATIE: Okay, Randy and I will meet you there as soon as we can. Bye!

ALLISON: Good-bye!

(Katie calls Randy.)

RANDY: Randy Zak here.

KATIE: Randy! It's Katie. We have a major problem. Sabrina dyed her hair!

RANDY: That's a problem? Lots of people dye their hair. I've been thinking of putting a purple streak in mine.

KATIE: No! She tried to dye her hair blond so she would look more like the Sandy character.

RANDY: So what happened?

KATIE: She has orange hair!

RANDY: Wow! That is definitely uncool. What is she going to do now?

KATIE: She doesn't know what to do. That's why I'm calling. Allison and I are going over to Sabs's house to see if we can figure something out. We have to find a way to get her hair back to its normal color!

RANDY: I used to dye all my friends' hair back in New York. I think I know how we can fix it.

KATIE: Do you really?

RANDY: I think so. You go on over to Sabs's house. I have to make a stop at the drugstore and then I'll be right over. I've got to hurry — the stores all close at seven.

KATIE: Great! See you in a few minutes.

RANDY: *Ciao!*

Chapter Seven

Allison and Katie did such a good job of convincing me that Randy would be able to fix my hair that by the time Randy got to my house I was almost calm. I noticed right away that Randy was carrying a box just like the one I had gotten from the drugstore.

"I don't want any more dye in my hair!" I told her quickly, throwing the towel back over my head.

"Relax, Sabs," Randy said. "I brought a deep conditioner and some dark burgundy hair dye. It's as close to your natural hair color as I could find." She opened up the boxes and pulled on a familiar pair of clear plastic gloves. "I used to do this all the time for my friends back in New York. I know all the directions by heart."

"Sabs, why did you dye your hair?" Allison wanted to know as Randy started working the dye into my orange mop.

"I really thought it would help if I looked like Sandy. Then Dr. Rossi would give *me* the part instead of Stacy Hansen," I explained miserably.

"You could have just worn the wig," Katie suggested.

"Not after that audition," I told her emphatically. "There's no way I'll ever wear that wig again."

"It did look pretty funny," Katie said with a giggle.

"Not as funny as orange hair, though," Randy teased, laughing. Katie and Al started giggling, too. I had to smile myself. Now that I knew Randy was going to fix it, I had to admit that the idea of having orange hair really was pretty funny.

"There! All done. You can look in the mirror now," Randy said a few minutes later, as she poured one final cup of water over my head to rinse out the last bit of conditioner.

I straightened up slowly in front of the mirror. Even though Randy seemed to know what she was doing, I was still nervous about what I was going to see. I gulped hard, took a deep breath, and looked . . .

. . . and my hair was the exact same color as it had always been — dark red!

"Oh, Randy! Thank you!" I cried, running over to give her a big hug. "I would have died without you!"

"You're welcome," said Randy with a twinkle in her eye. "Just promise me one thing."

"Anything," I said.

"Promise me you'll never try to dye your hair again."

"I won't! Not ever," I vowed. "I'm never even going to say the word 'dye' again!"

I walked my friends to the front door just in time to meet my parents coming home from dinner. What a close call! I was the luckiest person in the world to have friends like Randy, Allison, and Katie!

Later, on my way upstairs to bed, I noticed that the bathroom smelled a lot like a beauty shop. I opened the bathroom window, turned on the fan, and closed the door behind me. If I was lucky, the smell would be gone before anyone else went in. Exhausted, I went up the stairs to my room. I think I was asleep before my head hit the pillow. It had been a really tough day.

The next day was Saturday. Randy, Katie, Al, and I had all planned to meet at the mall to see a movie and go shopping.

As I was getting ready to go out, I realized that I still didn't look any more like Sandy than I had the day before. I had to do something soon, or I'd never get the part. I looked through some of my fashion magazines and decided that I should try changing my look from "sweet and innocent" to "sexy and sophisticated."

I started digging around in my underwear drawer, throwing things on the floor as I went through them.

"Aha! Finally," I said as I pulled out a pale pink training bra with a pink bow in the middle. The first thing I did was pull the childish pink bow off. Then I slipped the bra over my head. It wasn't the kind with hooks, but it would have to do.

Last year I had begged my mother to buy it for me, even though I didn't exactly need it. I had worn it once on the day I got it, but it was so uncomfortable I had never worn it again.

Then I slipped a white turtleneck on over the bra. I stood in front of my mirror, expecting to see a whole new me. Instead, I looked just like I always did. I definitely didn't look any older or more sophisticated. I had to do something more!

I went into the bathroom and grabbed two handfuls of tissues. They were blue tissues, but I figured that was okay. I stuffed a few into my bra and then looked in the mirror. Then I took a few more, and a few more. After a few more tissues, I looked at my reflection in the mirror and was finally satisfied. I looked much older already.

I put on my nicest jeans and my new tan boots with the one-inch heels. My mother won't let me wear any shoes with more than a one-inch heel until I'm older. By the time I'm old enough to wear real heels, they'll probably be out of style!

I fluffed up my hair and used some of my mom's mousse. Then I put on a little bit of pale pink lip gloss and sprayed on some baby powder cologne that my grandmother had given me. For the finishing touch, I put on a quick coat of pale pink nail polish.

I checked myself in the mirror one last time before I left for the mall. I thought I looked much more mature. I couldn't wait for my friends to see my new image!

My brother Luke, who's in high school, had promised to drive me to the mall. He was already waiting out front in his car. As I flew downstairs, I could hear him honking his horn.

We were halfway to the mall when I noticed that the sky was getting really dark. Then it began to rain. After a few minutes, the rain got heavier and heavier until it was coming down in sheets. Luke tried to drop me off really close to the door, but all the other drivers were trying to do the same thing. We could barely get near it. I just took a deep breath, opened the car door, and ran for the mall.

By the time I got into the mall, my hair was soaking wet and so were all my clothes. Then I looked down and saw bright blue, sopping wet tissues showing through my white turtleneck. I looked back up to see Katie, Allison, and Randy standing there. "Hi, guys," I said. My hair was wet, and my feet felt all squishy in my boots.

"Hi, Sabs," Katie said slowly, staring at my chest.

"Sabrina?" Allison said.

"What . . ." Randy began. She looked as if she was about to burst out laughing.

"What's the matter with your . . . shirt?" Katie asked finally, her eyes wide.

"It's my mature look," I explained quickly. "I wanted to look older, so I put on a bra. But it didn't make me look any different, so I . . . "

"You stuffed it with tissues!" Randy said, laughing. Then Allison and Katie were giggling, too.

"It's not that funny," I told them. "I didn't know it was going to rain. What am I going to do?"

"Sabs," Katie suggested between giggles, "why don't you go to the bathroom and get yourself . . . dried off." Randy started laughing all over again. She was laughing so hard she had to lean up against the wall to keep from falling.

"We can go and buy the tickets for the movie and meet you there," Allison said, smiling.

"Here," Randy offered between gasps for breath, "take my jacket."

"Okay," I agreed quickly, pulling Randy's leather jacket on over my soaking wet shirt. I walked toward the bathroom as fast as I could. Just outside the door I heard Stacy's annoyingly loud and fake giggle from inside the bathroom. Stacy was the last person I wanted to see right now. I frantically looked right and left. I didn't have enough time to get around the corner before she came out the bathroom door. I grabbed the handle of the door closest to me and jumped inside a small, dark, dusty room.

I closed the door behind me just as the bathroom door was flung open.

I felt around, found a light switch, and turned on the light. I was in a janitor's closet filled with brooms and mops. I heard Stacy's voice fade and decided it was safe to leave. But when I tried the door, nothing happened. I was locked in!

Now what was I going to do? I tried jiggling the lock, then ramming the door with my shoulder. But the door didn't even budge.

I moved to the back of the closet so I could run forward and give the door one last shove. *Bang*! The door swung open and I went flying into someone's arms! I looked up — it was Cameron Booth!

"Sabrina! What were you doing in there?"

he asked. "I heard the banging, so . . ."

"I-I —" I stuttered. I had always wanted to end up in Cameron's arms, but I had never pictured it like this! "I've got to go," I blurted out. Then I turned around and walked as quickly as I could down the hall before he noticed my blue chest.

I hid around the corner until he had left, then went into the bathroom and pulled all the dripping wet tissues out of my bra. I quickly dried my hair with the hot-air hand dryer, and finally I looked like myself again. I stopped and stared for a second at my reflection in the mirror.

"Well, Sabs," I murmured to myself. "I guess you'll have to get the part by being just the way you are."

Chapter Eight

Monday morning, I got up early so I could check the cast list before first period. I showered and dressed in the clothes I had picked out the night before — a light green drop-waisted dress with flowers all over it, white stockings, and green flats. Then I ate a quick breakfast and ran out the door. Halfway to school, I realized I had forgotten to read my horoscope. How could I forget my horoscope on what might be the most important day of my life?

Since I was pretty close to the little corner store on Main Street that sells newspapers, I ducked inside and bought one. I quickly flipped to the horoscope page. I know exactly where the horoscopes are, since I read them every day!

Pisces. The moon is in your sign today. Be sure to take advantage of what you have. That sounded good. I usually have a good day when the moon is in my sign. I continued on to school, feeling better already.

I was practically the first person in the whole building. I kept shifting from foot to foot impatiently while I waited outside the band room for Dr. Rossi to show up. Sunday had dragged by so slowly that I didn't think I could wait another minute to find out if I had gotten the part.

Finally Dr. Rossi arrived, but I didn't want to look too anxious by asking him right away whether I had gotten the lead.

"Hello, Dr. Rossi," I said, smiling at him.

"My, you're here early," he replied, smiling back.

"Yes, sir," I answered, wringing my hands behind my back. I was dying for him to take the list out of his briefcase. I guess he knew why I was there, because he took the cast list out before he had even unlocked the door.

"Congratulations, Sabrina," Dr. Rossi said to me as he stuck the cast list to the wooden door with a thumbtack. "I think you'll be the best Frenchy Acorn Falls has ever seen!"

"Frenchy!" I repeated, staring at the list in

disbelief. But there, under "Frenchy," was my name, Sabrina Wells. I looked a little farther up the list. Under "Sandy" was Stacy's name! Even worse, Cameron had gotten Danny's part!

Cameron and Stacy together for the whole six weeks of rehearsals? The thought was almost too much to handle. I turned away from the list. I couldn't even bear to see it in writing.

I managed to smile at Dr. Rossi. "Thank you," I mumbled and walked down the hall. When I turned the corner, I almost ran smack into Cameron.

"Hi, Sabrina. Is the cast list up yet?" he asked with a smile, his blue eyes twinkling.

"Ah, yeah, it is," I answered, hoping he wouldn't ask me which part I had gotten.

"So, what part did you get?" Cameron asked.

"Frenchy," I told him. I tried to sound happy and excited, but it took all of my acting talent just to keep a smile on my face.

"Wow, that's great! That's the second-biggest girl part in the play." He smiled. "You'll be terrific in that part!"

"Thanks," I said.

"Well, I'm going to go see what part I got.

Congratulations, Sabs," Cameron called out before he ran off to the music room.

I didn't even want to be in the play anymore. I didn't get the part I wanted, and Stacy — my enemy — was going to play the romantic lead with the guy I liked! I just wanted to go home and hide in my room and never hear the word *Grease* again. I walked slowly to my locker. There was Katie, taking her books out of the locker.

"Hi, Sabrina," Katie called down the hall to me.

"Hi, Katie," I mumbled.

"You didn't get it, did you?" she asked, after taking one look at my face.

"No, I got Frenchy." I frowned.

"That's great! Frenchy is a really big part!" Katie cried.

"But Stacy got Sandy," I moaned.

"Oh," Katie said sympathetically. She knew exactly what that meant. Stacy would be bragging all over the place, making sure everybody knew that she had gotten the lead in the school play.

"Well, we'd better go or we'll be late for class. Have a good day, Katie," I said quietly. I grabbed my math book from the pile in the bottom of our locker and walked to class. After math, Katie and I met at our locker and walked to band class together. Of course, we had to walk by Dr. Rossi's office to get there. The last thing I wanted to do was see that cast list again, so I zoomed past as if it wasn't even there.

I saw Cameron as soon as I sat down in the band room. He seemed really happy about getting his part. He was all smiles. People kept going up to him to congratulate him. Then I remembered that Sam, Nick, and Jason had been at the auditions, too. I hadn't even looked to see if they had gotten parts. At the end of class I got up my nerve to look at the cast list again.

Nick had gotten the part of Kenicke, and Jason had gotten Doody. Sam, my pain-in-the-neck brother, had gotten the part of Sonny. I guessed they must all be happy, since all they had wanted was to be in the play together.

I had a lot of trouble paying attention in English because I was thinking about the play. I was really surprised when the bell rang for homeroom. I listened to Mr. Hansen make his usual announcements, and then Ms. Staats told us that she had a surprise.

"Class, we will be having a special theme dance next month. The teachers have decided it would be appropriate to have a Sock Hop on the opening night of the school play, *Grease*.

"I don't know if any of you know what a Sock Hop is," Ms. Staats continued, "but we thought it would be fun if everyone dressed in clothes from the fifties."

She went to her desk and picked up a pile of papers. She handed a few to the first person in each row and asked them to pass them back after they had looked at them.

"These are some pictures of what the typical young women and men wore during the fifties. Of course, those of you who are in the play should wear your costumes," Ms. Staats told us.

"Now, tomorrow I'll be asking for volunteers for the decorating committee and the entertainment committee," Ms. Staats finished. She walked back to her desk and took out her attendance book. Everybody else started talking about the dance.

Usually I have a great time at the school dances, but somehow I just couldn't get excited about this one. I was too depressed about the play. Maybe I wouldn't go to the dance at all.

"A Sock Hop could be cool," Randy said from behind me. "They wore some pretty funky clothes in the fifties, believe it or not."

"Yeah," I answered.

"Hey, aren't you excited?" Randy asked, sounding surprised. "I mean, it'll be sort of like the whole school is throwing a party for the people in the play."

"I guess you're right," I answered her. Right then I didn't think anything having to do with the fifties or *Grease* could ever be fun.

Ms. Staats announced that we could have the rest of homeroom to ourselves, and Katie and Allison came over to Randy and me from their seats on the other side of the room.

"Wow! A Sock Hop! It sounds like so much fun!" Katie said, fixing the barrette that was holding her hair back.

"If they get a good band or D.J., it will be," Randy replied. I started to get the feeling that my friends were all trying to get me into this dance so I wouldn't be so upset about playing Frenchy instead of Sandy.

"Why don't we join the entertainment committee?" Allison suggested. "That way we can make sure we get a good band."

"Yeah! I don't think we'll have enough time to be on the decorating committee for the dance and the stage crew for the play," Katie agreed. "But we could help pick out the entertainment."

"Good idea," Randy agreed. She looked at me, waiting for me to agree, too.

"Okay," I finally said. I tried to smile, but I wasn't quite ready for that yet. I know I'm pretty dramatic about things sometimes, but that's just part of being an actress.

Homeroom finally ended, and we all went to lunch. I sat down to eat my lettuce and tomato sandwich. I noticed right away that my mother had packed cookies for me, too. I had told her that I only wanted to eat lettuce and tomato sandwiches for lunch because they were nutritious and low in calories. But Mom knows me too well. Those cookies were just what I needed in the middle of a tough day. *Thanks, Mom*, I thought to myself.

Randy sat opposite me eating her usual, a container of yogurt. Allison was having a ham and cheese sandwich on homemade bread that her grandmother had made. Katie was still on the lunch line.

Randy swallowed a spoonful of yogurt and said, "So, Sabs, when do rehearsals start?"

"Tomorrow," I told her shortly.

"You don't look very happy about it," Allison pointed out.

"I didn't get the lead!" I blurted out, staring at Stacy, who was sitting a few tables away from us. She was surrounded by her clique, and all of them were acting as if she'd just won an Academy Award or something. She was tossing her long blond hair around and talking in this high, phony voice.

"I worked so hard for that part," I mumbled.

"Come on, Sabs. Frenchy is the perfect part for you," Randy encouraged me.

"And we know that you're going to be so good that everyone will see what a great actress you are," Allison added.

"Do you really think so?" I asked, looking up at Randy.

Randy pushed a stray piece of long dark hair out of her eyes. "Would I lie to you?" she answered. "Anyway, anybody could play

Sandy. It takes a really awesome actress to play a character like Frenchy because she's so funny and different."

"But Stacy is even more stuck-up than ever since she got the part," I pointed out.

"She's not worth getting upset over," Randy said, dismissing the subject with a wave of her hand. Just then Katie sat down with her lunch tray.

"What is that orange stuff?" Randy asked curiously, wrinkling her nose.

Katie looked closer at the strangely colored blob on her plate. "It said 'macaroni and cheese' on the menu," she informed us.

"Well, it looks radioactive to me," Randy joked, scraping the bottom of her yogurt cup.

"Thanks, Randy," Katie replied with a giggle.

"Really," I echoed. "Maybe you'll turn into a mutant after you eat it."

Everybody laughed.

"So, Sabs, are you psyched to be Frenchy?" Katie asked a few minutes later.

"Yes, Katie, I guess I'm starting to get psyched." And believe it or not, I was!

Chapter Nine

Three o'clock. Why does the day always fly by when you don't want it to? Today was the first day of rehearsals, and I was really, really nervous. The closer it got to rehearsal time, the more jittery my stomach became.

I remembered what Randy and Allison had said at lunch the day before and held my head up high as I opened the door to the auditorium. I was wearing a really cool new dress that I'd gotten at my favorite store, Dare. It's dark green and has two tiers of ruffles at the bottom. When I turn around, the ruffles balloon around me. I think it's pretty cool. Plus, it's a known fact that green is a great color for redheads.

Randy, Katie, and Allison had to meet with the rest of the stage crew in the art room, so I made my entrance alone. Almost everyone else was already in the auditorium, and Dr. Rossi was passing out scripts.

I noticed Sam sitting with his friends in the far corner on one side of the auditorium, and Stacy and her group on the other. I definitely didn't want to sit with Stacy's friends, so I decided to sit with Sam.

I made a beeline in Sam's direction. I pushed my knapsack under an empty seat next to him. Then I looked around to see who else was there. I couldn't believe it. Sitting in the seat right next to Sam on the other side was Cameron Booth! I sat all the way back in my seat, hoping that Cameron wouldn't see me. Luckily Dr. Rossi chose that moment to start.

"Okay, everyone. Can I have your attention, please?" Dr. Rossi began. "I would like us all to read through the lines from the beginning. Of course, we will have to read from the scripts for the first week or so, but in two weeks, I would like you all to have your lines memorized."

"All the lines memorized in two weeks?" Sam whispered in horror. "I can't do that!"

I didn't see what the big deal was. Just from watching the movie three times, I already knew most of the lines — Sandy's and Frenchy's! I've always been good at learning things by heart, though. It's one of my strengths.

"Don't worry, Sam. Maybe you could invite your friends over, and we could all rehearse together. Like maybe Nick and Jason . . . and Cameron." I tried to say that last part as casually as possible. I hoped that Sam hadn't noticed that I was hinting. If he did notice and he figured out that I had a crush on Cameron, he would never stop teasing me!

"Hey, that's a great idea, Sabs," my brother whispered back. Actually, it was one of my better ideas, if I do say so myself.

The first day of rehearsals went pretty well, except for one thing. Frenchy is supposed to be Sandy's best friend in the play. Pretending to be Stacy's friend was probably going to be one of the biggest challenges of my life! If I pulled this one off, I deserved an Oscar! But that's the secret to being a great actress — making pretend stuff seem totally real. I knew I could do it. I'd just have to work really hard.

The whole cast read through the lines, sitting around on the stage. We didn't do any of the songs, though. In between the scenes where I had lines, I looked around at the rest of the cast.

Eva was playing Rizzo, and B.Z. had gotten the part of Jan, so Stacy had plenty of friends to talk to during rehearsals. In fact, there were only a few girls in the whole play who weren't in Stacy's clique: Donna DeAngeles, who was playing Patty Simcock, and Paige O'Leary, who played Miss McGee, the principal of Rydell High. I didn't really know any of them yet, but I had a feeling that we would have plenty of time to get to know one another over the next few weeks.

The first week flew by, and pretty soon we were reading the lines from our places on the stage. That's when it was time to learn the dance steps. I was really glad that Mom and Dad had taught me the hand jive. I had practiced it while I was watching the movie, too. It was really funny to watch twenty people trying to do the same movements together — and keep time with the music. Stacy kept getting totally confused. She was flapping her hands around like a bird, and she got so mad when Cameron tried to help her that she stomped off the stage. Sam looked so silly when he tried to do it. His arms and legs were all doing different things to a rhythm of their own. Nick even hit himself in the head once! But it was fun, and I noticed that people were trying so hard to get the dance routine that they became less nervous after a while.

Besides the hand jive, we had to learn other dances from the fifties, like the Stroll. All the couples lined up in two rows, and one couple danced down the center between them. The couple in the middle did some steps or twirls, or whatever they felt like doing. Each couple who went down the center was supposed to do something a little bit different. Then, when they had danced all the way through, they joined the two rows and the pair at the head of the line got their turn to dance through the center. It was a lot of fun, except that most of the time I had to dance with Sam because we are almost the same height. Stacy, of course, got to dance with Cameron, and Eva got to dance with Nick.

For the whole first week, I didn't get to see Allison, Randy, or Katie, because of rehearsals. At first they spent all of their time in the art room planning the scenery; then they did all of the actual painting and building backstage.

The set was starting to look really good. We had a cardboard car that was supposed to be

Greased Lightning, the car that Kenicke buys and fixes up in the play. It was red and had yellow flames painted on it. It looked awesome! Randy had done most of the painting. She's a really great artist. She must have inherited the talent from her mother.

We practiced every day after school for the next two weeks. Some days were better than others; sometimes some people did their parts better than other people — and sometimes vice versa. All in all, I loved every single second of rehearsals. I think being onstage and making an audience believe you are someone else is the most incredible experience in the world!

Finally, the following week on a Friday afternoon, Dr. Rossi told us that we would be practicing without our scripts for the first time the following Monday.

I had been rehearsing in my room every night after dinner, so I already knew my lines by heart. I also knew that Sam didn't know all of his cues yet, and I could tell that he was kind of worried. I didn't want to bring up my idea about inviting all of his friends over to practice again because I didn't want Sam to find out that I had a crush on Cameron.

I had decided instead to just invite Katie, Al, and Randy over for dinner that night. My parents were going out to dinner and a movie, so my mom had said we could order pizza. Thank goodness! Otherwise, Luke would have had to cook. The last time he made hamburgers, he cooked them so long that they turned all black and got hard. Sam called them "Luke's hockey pucks." After Mom heard that story, she started letting us order pizza when she and my dad went out.

I met everybody after rehearsal, and we walked over to my house. "Come on in, guys," I said, holding the back door open for my friends. I took off my boots and left them by the back door. Randy then took off her black lace-up granny shoes, Allison added her penny loafers to the pile, and then Katie tossed in her Keds. My mom likes us to take off our shoes before we enter the house. She says that with five kids, two adults, a dog, and lots of friends through here all the time, things can get awfully dirty if we're not all careful.

"Hey, whose shoes are those?" Randy asked, pointing at the shoes in the corner.

I looked at the extra-large pile. I didn't recognize any of the shoes, except for Sam's high-top sneakers with the yellow and purple stripes on them. But those white sneakers sure looked familiar. I knew I had seen them somewhere before. I just couldn't remember where.

We walked into the kitchen, talking about the play and how much we all had to do over the weekend. I guess none of us were paying attention, because we were all surprised to see who was sitting at the kitchen table. There were Sam and most of the male cast members from *Grease* — including Cameron — drinking milk and eating Mom's homemade oatmeal cookies! Now I remembered where I had seen those sneakers.

"Hi!" they all called out between mouthfuls of cookies. I was in total shock. I mean, I was used to seeing Nick and Jason in the kitchen because they're Sam's best friends, but this was incredible! Cameron Booth was in my kitchen! I could hardly keep the smile from my face.

"We're getting ready to order pizza for dinner," Sam informed me. "Should I get another one for you guys?" He stood up and started walking toward the phone in the hallway.

"Yeah, sure," I murmured. I was still in

shock at seeing Cameron Booth in my house.

"What do you want on it?" Sam called from the hall. He had the phone receiver in one hand and was stretching around the corner to look into the kitchen.

"Mushrooms," Katie told him. "And make sure they don't put any anchovies on it!" she added. Sam nodded and ducked back around the corner.

"We're here to memorize our lines," Nick was explaining to Randy and Allison. Nick and I are pretty good friends. At one point at the beginning of the year, I thought I liked him, but that was a long time ago. It was nothing like the crush I have on Cameron.

"I'm really glad you guys are here," Cameron said, turning to me. He was glad to see me! *Wow*! All of a sudden I was so happy that I started to blush, of course. I noticed that Cameron was sitting in my usual seat at the kitchen table. It had to be fate. Now I would never sit in that seat again without thinking of him.

"We were also just fighting over who would have to read the girls' lines," Cameron continued with a grin.

Randy started to laugh. "I would have loved to see that — the all-male version of *Grease*. Only in Acorn Falls!" she joked. "It would be like 'Monty Python' or something."

Nick had his nose buried in the script. Allison was reading it over his shoulder.

"I'm in really big trouble," Nick moaned. "I don't know anything!"

"Oh, yes, you do!" I insisted. "You always do well at rehearsals."

"But there's no way I can do it without the book," he said, frustrated.

"We'll just keep going over it tonight until you know it," said Sam, walking back into the kitchen. "Let's start while we're waiting for the pizzas."

"Right. We need all the help we can get, if we're going to have the whole play memorized by Monday." Cameron sighed.

Allison, always the logical one, said, "You'll probably be able to remember it better if you do the whole thing. I mean, the acting and the dancing along with the lines."

"That's a good idea," I said quickly. "Why don't we all go into the family room. There's a lot more space there."

"We even have the sound track, so we can practice the dancing scenes," Sam put in. "Come on, Nick. Let's go get the stereo from my room and bring it down here."

The two of them ran up the stairs and the rest of the group moved into the family room. This was almost like a party. And Cameron Booth was actually in my house!

As soon as Sam and Nick came back, we started going over and over the scenes until even Allison, Randy, and Katie knew the lines by heart. I had really wanted to read Sandy's part, but Sam said I should just keep reading my own so that I didn't confuse everybody. So Katie read for Sandy, Randy read for Rizzo, and Allison read for Marty, Jan, and Patty Simcock.

There weren't enough girls for the dance scene, so we just practiced the hand jive a couple of times. Allison got the idea to start it out really slow, counting out loud as we made each movement. When everybody had it down correctly at one speed, we would start counting faster. Pretty soon, we were jiving to the music — and I'm sure we looked just as good as the characters in the movie!

We were all getting the hang of it when the

doorbell rang. It was good to stop for a while and eat pizza and catch our breaths. When I sat down on the floor of the living room with my first slice, Cameron came over and sat down next to me with his pizza. Having him so close made me so nervous, I could hardly eat. It felt almost like a first date or something. Katie kept looking over at me and winking when nobody was looking. Every time she did it, I felt my body blush starting up again.

After we finished the pizza, we decided to run through the whole play once without looking at our scripts at all. Mark and Luke came home just in time to be our audience. We went all the way from the first line to the last — except for the dances — without one mistake. Mark and Luke were really impressed. They even applauded and said that we were terrific!

When my parents came home from their dinner and movie, the whole group of us were sprawled all over the family room, gasping. We had just finished doing the hand jive at top speed. Everyone was surprised when my dad told us it was ten o'clock. We'd been having such a good time that none of us had noticed how late it was. Then Dad offered to drive everyone home, and the rehearsal party broke up. It had been a great night.

I spent the rest of that weekend trying to catch up on all the homework I hadn't exactly been keeping up with since rehearsals started. Once or twice Sam and I would listen to each other say our lines without the scripts. Finally both of us were satisfied that we wouldn't disappoint Dr. Rossi on Monday.

On Sunday night I dreamed that I was sitting next to Cameron in Greased Lightning, eating pizza and doing the hand jive at the same time. I kept tossing tomato sauce on his sweater by mistake, no matter how hard I tried not to. Finally he got out of the car and walked over to Stacy's house instead of mine.

On my way to rehearsal Monday afternoon, I decided it was time to give up my script. I walked into the auditorium, smiled at Dr. Rossi, and put my script on the top of the pile at the edge of the stage. I felt really proud when I saw Sam come up and put his script on the pile, too.

Stacy walked confidently into the auditorium wearing blue overalls, a pink cotton shirt, and pink flats. She pulled out her script, opened it to the first page, and stood at her mark on the stage.

"Excuse me, Stacy. Could you put the script away, please," Dr. Rossi instructed her. "As I told you on Friday, we'll be doing the play from memory today."

"But I have to use my script, Dr. Rossi. I don't know everything by heart yet. After all, I do have the biggest part," Stacy protested, raising one eyebrow and looking at Dr. Rossi as if what she was saying was totally logical and obvious.

"Just try it without the script," Dr. Rossi said patiently. "I'm sure you know more than you think you do. No one is expected to be perfect today." Stacy made a face and slammed her script down on top of the pile.

One great thing about being Frenchy is that she has the very first line in the play. I took a deep breath and read my line.

"Oh, I, uh . . ." Stacy finally stammered.

"'I met a boy at the beach,'" Katie whispered from behind the curtain where she was painting a "Rydell High School" sign.

Stacy shot a nasty look toward the curtain.

"'I met a boy at the beach,'" she repeated. It

was hard not to enjoy the fact that Stacy wasn't prepared. We had all worked so hard to memorize our lines perfectly that there was no way we were going to let her get away with not knowing hers. I read my lines and smiled at her sweetly, knowing it was only going to make her even more angry.

We finished our scene and then it was the guys' turn. I crossed my fingers and hoped they remembered all the things we had rehearsed the other night.

Sam, Nick, and Cameron made it all the way through their scene without missing even one word.The only person who had made a mistake was Stacy! Stacy the Great didn't sound so great after all!

We went right into the first song, and I sang my one solo line. I sounded perfect, since Frenchy is supposed to be off-key!

The rehearsal went really well until Stacy forgot another line, and Cameron had to tell her what it was. Stacy acted as if she couldn't believe that Cameron knew all of her lines as well as all of his own. She tried to tell us again that her part was so much more important than any of ours that we couldn't expect her to know all of her lines yet. But Cameron's part was as big as hers, and he knew all of his lines — and most of hers. So Stacy wasn't fooling any of us.

Eva made a few mistakes, too. At the end of the rehearsal, Dr. Rossi told all of us that we had done very well. But then he asked Eva and Stacy to stay for a few extra minutes. Practice definitely does make perfect. All of that rehearsing Friday night had really paid off.

As I walked out of the auditorium, I remembered that I had left my script on the stage. I still needed it to learn some of the gestures and facial expressions that Dr. Rossi had suggested, so I had to go back and get it. As I walked across the stage, I just happened to hear Dr. Rossi telling Eva and Stacy that he didn't think that they were trying quite as hard as the rest of the cast and that they should practice a little more to catch up with the rest of us. Stacy looked mad enough to start screaming right then and there. When Dr. Rossi dismissed them, she stomped out of the auditorium so hard that the floor shook.

Wow! What would happen if Stacy got so mad that she quit the show? I might be able to take her place! But then who would play Frenchy, I thought. I had to admit that I actually kind of liked being Frenchy.

One week later, the cast was waiting for rehearsal to begin, when Dr. Rossi walked in and said he had an announcement to make.

"I am very sorry to say that we have lost one of our cast members," Dr. Rossi began.

I looked around and saw that Stacy wasn't there! Had she really decided to quit? Or had Dr. Rossi kicked her out of the play?

"Lisa Ryan hasn't been feeling very well lately, and her doctor says she has to have her tonsils out. Unfortunately, this means that she can't be in the play."

Just then Stacy walked down the aisle. What was I thinking? Stacy would never give up her role as Sandy no matter how mad she got. She'd never be able to handle someone else having her part. I'd forgotten that she was always late for rehearsal.

"Now, opening night is only a week and a half away, and we don't have a Marty. Does anyone have any suggestions?" Dr. Rossi asked.

Suddenly I had an awesome idea!

I raised my hand as high as I could. "Could Katie Campbell play Marty?" I asked breathlessly. I always get a little breathless when I'm excited about something. "She knows all the lines from helping me study," I assured Dr. Rossi.

Katie raised her head from the sign she was painting.

"What?" she cried. She looked totally shocked. She also looked as if she wanted to kill me!

"Well, I haven't heard you read, Katie," Dr. Rossi said to her, "but it wouldn't hurt to give it a try for today, would it?"

"Well," Katie began, "I guess that would be okay. But —"

"It's just a trial, Katie," Dr. Rossi said soothingly. "We'll talk about whether you want to actually be in the play after the rehearsal, okay?"

Katie nodded.

"Yay!" I shouted, jumping up and down.

Dr. Rossi started the rehearsal a few minutes later. He let Katie use a copy of the script, but she only had to check it once or twice. She really did know Marty's part very well.

"Thanks a lot, Sabs!" Katie joked, as she walked out of the auditorium to where Randy, Allison, and I were waiting for her. She had stayed after rehearsal to talk with Dr. Rossi about being in the show.

"Are you going to do it?" I asked excitedly. "Please tell me you said yes! I know he asked you to do it!"

"I said yes," Katie said, laughing. "It wasn't like I really had a choice or anything!"

"We're going to have so much fun!" I cried.

"Yeah," Katie said, her eyes shining. "Acting on the stage is a lot different from acting in your family room, Sabs."

"Well, I'm glad you didn't volunteer me," Randy said as we walked out of the school.

"Me, too!" Allison agreed. If you ask me, Allison would make a great actress. I would have to talk her into being in the next play.

"Oh! I almost forgot to tell you. We found this cool D.J. for the Sock Hop," Randy exclaimed.

"Who is he?" I asked.

"His name's D.J. Doug," Katie began.

"Nice name," I teased.

"He's really good, though! He plays all the oldies — songs from the fifties — and he only costs a hundred dollars!" Katie told me enthusiastically.

"He is totally cool," Randy agreed. "He knows all about the great all-time drummers like Buddy Rich, and he's going to let me help set up his equipment."

"Now all we have to do is get Ms. Staats to approve him," I said.

"No problem!" Allison jumped in. "D.J. Doug played at her niece's sweet-sixteen party. Ms. Staats loves him!"

"Great! The dance is really shaping up. But what about the decorations?" I asked. We weren't actually on the decorating committee, but I wanted to make sure that they were doing a good job. If they didn't, it could ruin the whole dance! "I wish there were two of me so that I could be in the play and be in charge of the decorations, too," I sighed.

Allison, Randy, and Katie burst out laughing.

"Oh, no! Just imagine what it would be like if there were two Sabrina Wellses in the world," Katie cried in mock horror.

"No cute guy would be safe," Randy teased.

"And neither would any of the clothing stores in Minnesota," Allison added, giggling.

I had to laugh. They were right. If one of me was always running in twenty different directions, two of me would be running in forty different directions. I wouldn't be able to keep up! Besides, one of me was probably all that Acorn Falls could handle!

"I wonder who's in charge of the decorations, anyway," Katie asked as soon as we had all caught our breaths.

"Winslow Barton's the head of the committee," Allison replied.

"Winslow! Oh, no!" I moaned.

A lot of kids at Bradley think that Winslow is the class nerd. I got to know him pretty well, though, when we worked on a project together for social studies this year, and he's actually a really nice guy. But he is kind of strange. I had to wonder what kind of decorations he was going to come up with.

"Hey! He's doing an awesome job," Randy broke in. "He told me all about what he's planning when I saw him in study hall the other day. He's going to blow up pictures of people and things that were really popular during the fifties, like James Dean, old cars, drive-ins, soda shops, and stuff. And there'll be lots of balloons and streamers, like there are in the dance in *Grease*," she explained.

Randy and Winslow have been friends since the beginning of the year, when she first moved here. They both like computers and music a lot, and Randy is always going over to the Bartons' house to try out new computer programs.

By then we had reached Elm Park, the place where we have to split up to go to our different houses.

"You know, I think Winslow's idea sounds pretty good," I told Randy. Now I could relax about the decorations, too, and just concentrate on the play.

We all said good-bye, and I walked the rest of the way home, going over my lines in my head. I had to remember to call Katie later and make sure she was studying hers, too. After all, we only had a week and a half left until opening night!

Chapter Ten

When the play was only one week away, Dr. Rossi announced we were having a dress rehearsal the following Monday. I already had part of my costume, but I needed something for the dance scene, and Katie needed two costumes to wear.

Katie and I decided to ask my mother if we could raid the trunks of old clothes up in our attic over the weekend. My mother never throws anything away — especially clothes. She's always saying that styles go in cycles and that someday we'll be glad she kept all of that stuff. Every summer my dad says that we should have a garage sale, but we never do.

Anyway, Katie came over on Saturday, and we went up to the attic storage room next to my bedroom. We started rummaging through boxes and bags. We found my baby book, with pictures of me and Sam when we were babies.

We found Mom's wedding dress and my grandfather's violin. Finally, after about two hours, we got around to opening the huge trunk full of old clothes.

"Wow! This is perfect," I cried when we pulled two totally gorgeous dresses out of the trunk. One of them was robin's-egg blue with short, puffy sleeves and a row of lace at the bottom. Katie's eyes opened really wide as soon as she saw it.

"Oh, Sabs. Look at this," she whispered. She held the dress up against herself.

"You would look so good in that dress," I told her. "I think it would be just perfect for the dance scene."

"Do you really think your mom would let me borrow it?" Katie asked anxiously.

"Of course she will," I assured her. "She said we could use anything we found."

The second dress was dark green with a wide skirt and spaghetti straps. I absolutely loved it. I already had the perfect pair of pumps to go with it, too. Katie and I gathered up the two dresses and ran over to my room to try them on. We were standing in front of the mirror, practicing the hand jive in our dresses, when I suddenly remembered that we had something else we had to do today.

"Ohmygosh!" I clamped my hands over my mouth. "What time is it?" I cried. We had gotten so excited about the dresses that both Katie and I had forgotten the time. A lot of the girls in the play are in this group called the Pink Ladies, just like the guys are in a group called the T-Birds. Dr. Rossi had ordered a "Pink Ladies" jacket for each of the female characters who needed them, and today was the day we were supposed to pick them up.

"It's three o'clock," Katie told me, glancing down at her watch.

"We have to go! Quick! The T-Shirt Shoppe is only open until four on Saturdays!" I exclaimed. "We've absolutely got to have our jackets for the dress rehearsal."

Katie and I changed back into our regular clothes as fast as we could and ran down the stairs, out the door, and up the block toward Main Street. We made it to the store in plenty of time. I could see the jackets hanging right behind the counter.

The jackets were pale pink cotton with the words "Pink Ladies" written in big black script letters on the back. Mine had "Frenchy" embroidered on the front lapel, and Katie's, of course, said "Marty."

"Aren't they cool!" I gushed, putting mine on right there in the store. They looked exactly like the ones from the movie!

"Humph!" I heard Stacy snort from behind me. I turned to find her examining my outfit from head to toe. "I'll take mine," Stacy ordered the clerk, still staring at me. "It's the one that says 'Sandy' on it."

Stacy is so rude sometimes!

Stacy looked her jacket over with a frown. "I don't know why Dr. Rossi insisted that mine be the same as everyone else's," she complained. "I told him that it should be different — maybe satin instead of cotton. After all, I *am* the lead," she went on, flipping her blond hair over her shoulder.

"After all, I *am* the lead," seemed to be the only thing that Stacy said anymore.

"Have you learned all of your lines yet, Stacy?" Katie asked with a smile.

"That was great!" I complimented Katie, giggling after Stacy had stormed out of the store without a word. Sometimes Katie really

comes through. After that, the two of us head-
ed back toward my house.

"What are you going to wear for the rest of
the show, Katie?" I asked. "And what are Al
and Randy wearing to the Sock Hop?"

"I don't know. Maybe my mother has some
of her old clothes, too," Katie replied. "I'll have
to ask her."

"Be serious! Your mother throws things out
before they even have a chance to get old!" I
said, laughing.

"Yeah, you're right," Katie sighed, nodding.
"Why don't we go over to Randy's and see if
she has any ideas," she suggested.

As we walked, I helped Katie practice her
lines and we went over the words to all of the
songs. A few minutes later, we were walking
up the path to the renovated barn where Randy
and her mother live.

Olivia — Randy's mom told all of us to call
her by her first name — let us into the house
and told us that Randy was in the living room
watching one of the *Halloween* movies. Randy
just loves horror movies. Randy waited until
Michael Myers had finished off some poor girl
in a nightgown before she turned to us.

"What's up, guys?" she asked. Randy was wearing an extra-large black sweatshirt and a pair of multicolored biker shorts.

"We came over to ask what you and Allison are going to wear to the Sock Hop," Katie explained.

"And we need your help to figure out what Katie is going to wear for the play," I added. I love to plan outfits, but Randy has some of the coolest ideas about clothes. She thinks up the most bizarre combinations, and what's really weird is that they usually look good.

"Don't worry. I have an idea," Randy said. She sprang off the couch and ran into the kitchen. Randy's house is a converted barn. It's really one big room with a screen in front of her mother's room, and a little loft that Randy uses as her bedroom.

Katie looked at me and shrugged.

When Randy came back, she was carrying the phone book. She opened it to the Yellow Pages and read aloud to us, "Used and Vintage Clothes — The Opportunity Shop, Quentin Street, Acorn Falls."

"Vintage clothes?" I repeated, not really knowing exactly what they were.

"It's kind of like an antique store for clothes," Katie explained.

"I'll call Allison. Let's hurry over there right now. They're open until six," Randy said, running to the phone.

Allison said she would meet us at The Opportunity Shop, so we said good-bye to Randy's mom and hurried over to the store. I was starting to wish that I had brought my bike. We had been running all over Acorn Falls.

We had no trouble meeting Allison at The Opportunity Shop. It turned out to be a little shop stuck between a hardware store and a florist shop on Quentin Street. I had never really noticed it before.

"Wow! Look at all these old clothes," I exclaimed, looking around the store in awe. It was incredible. I'd never seen a store with so much clothing packed into such a small space. The best part was that everything was heaped in messy piles on tables and racks. You definitely didn't have to worry about making a mess there.

"Look at this old scarf. It's only fifty cents! I can wear it with my "Pink Ladies" jacket for the play," Katie said excitedly, waving a hot pink silk scarf around.

"These pants are so cool," Randy called from a table near the back of the store. She was holding up a pair of black cropped wool pants that looked just like something out of this month's *Young Chic* magazine.

"Those were called Capri pants back in the fifties," the owner of the shop said as she walked out of the back room. "Marilyn Monroe used to wear black Capri pants all the time."

"The fifties! Then I can wear these for the Sock Hop!" Randy exclaimed. I could tell that she was really glad not to have to wear a poodle skirt, or something boring like that.

"I'm Mrs. Johnson," the owner said, smiling at us. I guess I had kind of expected her to be an old lady, since she was selling vintage clothing, but she had long brown hair hanging all the way down her back, and she was wearing a cool drop-waisted yellow dress with yellow rhinestone jewelry. It looked hip and old-fashioned at the same time, yet somehow it was perfect on her. "If there's anything I can do to help, just let me know," she added softly.

All of a sudden, Allison walked up to us holding this long purple skirt with a fluffy white poodle on it.

"Hey, it's just like mine, but it's purple!" I exclaimed.

"I have to get this," Allison gasped, between giggles. "It's so funny!"

Allison is really tall and she has a good figure. I just knew she would look perfect in that purple poodle skirt.

Randy started rummaging through the racks along one wall, trying to find something to wear with her new old pants.

"How about this?" Mrs. Johnson offered, pulling a sweater out from the bottom of a pile on a table in front of her.

Randy held the avocado-colored cardigan sweater with pearl buttons up to herself.

"Wild," she said. "It's perfect."

"Well, almost," Mrs. Johnson corrected her. "The buttons are supposed to go in the back."

"In the back?" I asked. People in the fifties sure had some strange ideas!

"This is awesome," Randy said enthusiastically. "I even have a pair of black flats to go with this."

Now that Randy was all set, we had to finish Allison's and Katie's outfits.

With Mrs. Johnson's help, we found a white cotton shirt with a big black "L" sewn on the front. Mrs. Johnson swore that it was authentic. It went perfectly with Allison's poodle skirt.

We finally found an ankle-length straight blue skirt and a plain white sweater that looked just right with the pink scarf tied around Katie's neck.

Randy made us promise to come back to The Opportunity Shop again with her. She said it made her feel as if she was back in Greenwich Village in New York City, where they have lots of vintage clothes stores.

When I got back to my house, I found my parents sitting on the floor in the family room, surrounded by hundreds of old pictures and photo albums. "Hi, Mom. Hi, Dad. What happened in here?" I asked.

"After you left, I decided to go through those old trunks myself. Look what I found!" my mother told me, proudly motioning to the stacks of dusty photos on the floor.

"Come here, Sabs, and see how beautiful your mom looked on the day I took her to the senior prom," Dad said, smiling.

I sat down to look at the pictures with them.

It was weird for me to think that Mom and Dad were once in school and had crushes on each other. It's even harder to believe that they were ever my age. Actually, I've seen pictures of Mom when she was my age, and she looks just like me.

I was having fun sitting there looking at their old pictures when my mother sprang some news on me.

"Sabrina, I have something to tell you. Your father and I have volunteered to be chaperons for your Sock Hop!" Mom announced with a big smile.

Chaperons for my Sock Hop? The same Sock Hop where I was hoping and dreaming of maybe dancing with Cameron? I couldn't believe it! How could they do this to me? I mean, I love my parents, but enough is enough. Parents and social lives are like oil and water. They don't mix well. I had to think of a way to get out of this situation without hurting their feelings. But they looked so excited that I couldn't think of anything to say!

"Um . . . I . . . that's really nice, Mom," I stuttered. "I just remembered that I have to call Katie."

I ran to the phone by the staircase. This situation was too much for me to handle. I needed help! I dialed Katie's number as fast as I could and waited for her to pick up the phone.

"Hello!" said Katie cheerfully.

"Katie! It's Sabs. You won't believe this! My parents are going to chaperon the Sock Hop!" I whispered. I didn't want my parents to hear me.

"That's great!" Katie replied. "Your parents will make awesome chaperons. Why do you sound so upset?"

"What do you mean, 'That's great?'" I asked. "I don't want my parents to see me dancing with guys! They'll probably want me to stay and talk to them all night! How am I going to spend time with you and Al and Randy?"

"Sabs! You're getting all upset over nothing. I'm sure your parents won't want you to do that," Katie said reassuringly. "Anyway, what about Sam? How does he feel about it?"

"I don't know," I replied. "I haven't talked to him yet. I'd better do that — soon."

"Don't worry," Katie repeated.

"I'll try not to," I answered. I hung up the

phone and went upstairs to my room. I still couldn't believe that my parents were going to chaperon what was probably going to be the best dance of the year. I hoped Katie was right and that I was just getting upset over nothing.

Chapter Eleven

"Ohmygosh, Katie! I can't go onstage tonight!" I cried.

"What's wrong?" Katie asked nervously.

"Maybe the lights will go out during the play. Maybe I'll forget all my lines and my acting career will be over," I said, starting to get more and more nervous.

"Relax, Sabs!" Katie said calmly. "Just finish putting on your makeup, and we'll walk down to the soda machine and get something to drink."

When Katie and I walked out of the dressing room, we met Stacy. She must have seen the scared look on my face.

"What's the matter, Sabrina? Got a case of stage fright?" Stacy asked. "Well, you don't have to worry because everyone will be too busy watching me," she bragged. "Oh, I'd better go. There's a reporter waiting to take a picture of Cameron and me for tomorrow's newspaper." With that Stacy turned and walked away, flipping her long blond ponytail around like crazy.

"Ooh! She makes me mad!" I said to Katie, gritting my teeth. If only I could have thought of a comeback!

As Katie and I made our way through the crowded backstage, we suddenly heard someone call out, "Break a leg, you two!"

I looked up to see Randy and Allison waving at us. Just then I tripped. My mother's clunky old saddle shoes were really hard to get used to. I would have fallen if Katie hadn't grabbed my arm.

"It's just an expression," Randy called from the spotlight rigging, laughing. "I didn't really mean that you should do it."

I retied my shoelaces even tighter than before and ran to the cafeteria with Katie for a soda. When we returned backstage, we tried to peek out at the audience from behind the curtain. Suddenly my brother Sam came up behind us and scared me to death.

"Hey!" Sam said in a stage whisper. "Remember what Dr. Rossi said: 'If you can see them, they can see you.'" Sam shook his finger at us.

"Okay, okay." Katie laughed. Considering the fact that Katie hadn't really wanted to be in this play in the first place, she was doing great. She was so calm! I couldn't understand it at all. Katie practically pried my fingers from the curtain and led me back to the cast room. Every person in the room — even Stacy — looked tense and excited at the same time.

After what seemed like forever, we heard the band start to play the Rydell High School fight song from the play. That was our cue to take our places.

"Good luck!" Katie whispered, giving me a hug.

"Good luck!" I whispered, hugging her back.

"You guys are going to be great," a familiar voice said from behind us. I turned around and squinted in the darkness until my eyes found Allison, all dressed in black.

"Thanks," I whispered. Then the curtain opened and we sang the opening song. Actually, my voice squeaked because I was so nervous. Luckily, that was right in character for

Frenchy. I was trying very hard to forget that I was actually onstage in front of a live audience. I said my first line and waited for Stacy's reply.

"Oh, I . . ." Stacy hesitated and we all held our breath. "I met a boy at the beach," she finished, triumphantly. Then everyone started to breathe again.

Everybody said the right lines on cue. We were much better than we had been at the dress rehearsal. Dr. Rossi had said that a bad dress rehearsal meant a good opening night. I guess he was right. The rehearsal hadn't gone very well at all. We had all been so nervous that we kept messing up the dances and the songs — I even messed up one of my lines! But tonight we were really good.

Finally it was time for my big scene. Frenchy has dropped out of high school to go to beauty school, but now she's even failing that. Then she dyes her hair pink by mistake in tinting class. It's my favorite scene in the whole play.

The pink wig I had to wear over my own hair felt hot and itchy under all the lights on the stage. I was dying to scratch my head, but I couldn't. Instead, I just concentrated on my lines and tried to ignore the itching. The curtain opened, and the audience roared with laughter at my pink hair. Imagine what they would have done if they had seen my orange hair!

The scene takes place in a soda shop. Frenchy is sitting all alone, thinking about what a mess her life is, when suddenly her guardian angel appears. I think that's the best part. The stage crew had rigged it so that my guardian angel actually flew onto the stage! He swung in on some wires hooked to the catwalk above the stage.

The angel was played by Mr. Grey, our social studies teacher. He's the youngest and coolest teacher at Bradley, and all the girls thought that he was the perfect choice to make a guest appearance in the show.

The scene had worked really well in rehearsal. Mr. Grey had swung gently over my head and then landed beside me. Then he had sung his song and flown off again. This time, though, something went wrong. Mr. Grey swung halfway down and stopped. He was just hanging there, suspended in midair.

I almost panicked. I was about to run and grab his swinging feet when I noticed that the audience was clapping wildly. They didn't know that anything was wrong! I kept still, looking up at my guardian angel, and he sang his song while hanging in the air. He was swinging just a little bit, but I don't think the audience noticed. I thought the swinging made him look just like a real angel. It was great!

Randy was working the spotlight. She swung the light up to where Mr. Grey was hanging. It looked terrific, and the audience loved it. As Mr. Grey moved offstage, I had to wait a long time for the applause to die down so I could say my next line.

The slumber party scene went well, too. I'm supposed to pierce Sandy's ears, but she faints before I can finish. I don't have to tell you why it's one of my absolutely favorite scenes.

It was an awesome feeling to be in front of an audience. Lines that didn't sound the least bit funny to any of us during rehearsal made the audience roar with laughter. There is absolutely nothing like being onstage. It's an even better feeling than getting an A on a test. It made me feel almost as if a guy I liked had just smiled at me, but it wasn't nearly as embarrassing. I loved it!

And I think that acting loved me, too. I know the audience did! At the end, during the curtain calls, I got a standing ovation! I was so shocked that I just kind of stood there with my mouth open. Sam, was standing next to me, whispering, "Bow again!" So I did. The audience clapped and cheered and whistled so loudly, I thought the roof was going to cave in!

Stacy looked at me angrily. She was so mad that she didn't even smile during her curtain call.

At the very end, Dr. Rossi presented Stacy with a bouquet of flowers. The female lead always gets flowers at the end of opening night. But Stacy was so mad that I had gotten more applause than she had that she dumped her flowers in the garbage pail backstage.

Suddenly Katie was standing next to me. "You were great!" she exclaimed.

"Thanks! So were you," I told her. The next thing I knew, I was completely surrounded with people. My whole family, Randy, Allison, Dr. Rossi, and a lot of other people I didn't even know had come up to congratulate me. My father gave me a kiss and handed me two red roses. I buried my nose in them and smelled how sweet they were.

"From your mother and me," he said with a smile.

I gave him a big hug. "Thanks, Dad."

Right then I was so happy that I didn't even care that my parents were chaperoning the Sock Hop — or that Stacy had had the lead. I, Sabrina Wells, had stolen the show. Not to brag or anything, but you know how you just know when you've done something well? Nobody has to tell you — you just know.

Katie and I ran back to the dressing room to wash off all our stage makeup. I carefully put my flowers in a cup of water so that they would last. I was going to press them in my scrapbook when I got home. It would be fun to look back at them when I was a famous actress.

Allison and Randy came with us to change into their fifties clothes for the dance. Allison put on her poodle skirt and the white initial shirt. She loosened her hair from her braid and tied it up in a ponytail with a chiffon scarf. She looked just like one of the pictures Ms. Staats had shown us of teenagers in the fifties!

Randy put on her Capri pants and sweater, and her cat's-eye glasses. When we had finished getting dressed, we all looked as though we had gone through a time warp.

We walked over to the gym, where the dance was being held. We could hear the music all the way down the hall. As soon as we got to the doorway, I stopped walking. I couldn't believe what I was seeing. My mother was standing there in her old high school prom dress, and my father had his hair slicked back on the sides. He was wearing an old-fashioned pair of shoes with pointy toes, and the collar of his shirt was pulled up in the back.

"Sabs, you have the coolest parents in the world," Katie said from behind me. "I could never get my mother to do something like this."

"Mine either," Al agreed.

My parents saw me and just smiled and waved. They didn't run over and try to talk to me or embarrass me or anything. They looked like they were having a great time talking to the teachers and the other chaperons.

"Hey, Sabs! You were fantastic!" someone called out.

I turned around to see Cameron, still in his costume, walking toward me. He looked great with his blond hair slicked back like Danny's was supposed to be.

"You were fantastic, too," I told him.

"Come on. Let's dance the first dance," he said, grabbing my hand and pulling me into the gym. I looked around. The decorations were super-cool! On the walls there were all kinds of huge pictures, just like Randy had described. There was a TV and a VCR in each corner of the room, all of them showing the movie *Grease*. There were hundreds of balloons of all colors covering the ceiling and yards of streamers hanging on the walls. D.J. Doug had set up his equipment against one wall, and there was a punch table on the other side of the gym. Winslow had done a really great job as head of the decorating committee!

D.J. Doug was playing a cha-cha, one of the dances that Cameron and I had learned from being in the play. I couldn't believe I was actually dancing in Cameron's arms. Before we knew it, we had danced for half an hour straight, to a whole bunch of great fifties songs.

"Cameron, I have to get some punch," I gasped. I was completely out of breath from all the dancing.

"Me, too," he yelled over the music.

We wove our way through the crowd on the dance floor toward the punch bowl. Katie and Sam were already there. They had been dancing, too. Cameron and I got ourselves something to drink and then walked over to talk to them.

"Okay, kids. Time for a slow one," D.J. Doug announced. The lights in the gym were dimmed, and he started playing "Blue Moon." Cameron heard the first few notes and handed me his punch cup.

"I've gotta go," he muttered quickly and walked away toward the dance floor. I was really confused.

"Look!" Katie exclaimed, pointing to the far corner of the gym. I spun around and saw Cameron, Sam, Nick, and Jason on the bleachers, their backs to us and their pants around their ankles! It was just like what had happened at the dance in the movie, except that the guys were wearing boxer shorts that spelled out 'GREASE'.

The spotlight near D.J. Doug's table turned to shine on the four guys on the bleachers and everyone laughed and cheered. Eventually the guys left the bleachers giving each other the high-five as if they had just won a football game or something. Then Cameron came back across the gym to me.

"I'm sorry I had to run like that. The D.J. wasn't supposed to play that until later," he apologized.

"That's okay," I said. I was so happy to find out he hadn't gone to dance with anyone else that I couldn't help but smile. Cameron grinned back at me.

"Wanna dance some more?" he asked.

Just at that moment D.J. Doug put on another slow song, and I felt like running over and giving him a big hug.

"Sabs, I . . ."

I looked at him, puzzled. What was he trying to say?

"I think you have the prettiest hair in school," Cameron blurted out at last. I couldn't be sure in the dim lighting, but he might even have been blushing! I almost started to giggle, but I controlled myself. Here I had gone and dyed my hair so I could look like Stacy — but a super-cute guy liked it just the way it was! So even though I hadn't gotten the lead, everything had turned out better than I could possibly have imagined.

Someone was moving the spotlight around the dance floor, stopping it for a second on each of the couples. Pretty soon it was our turn, and the light hit me right in the eye.

"Who is that?" I asked, squinting and shading my eyes with one hand.

"I think it's Jason," Cameron told me, laughing. He made some kind of hand motion behind his back and the spotlight went out. In the sudden darkness, he leaned over and quickly kissed me on the cheek.

I noticed that Katie and Sam were dancing right next to us. Katie must have noticed the kiss because she was smiling right at me.

As I looked around to see if Randy and Allison had also seen Cameron kiss me, I noticed Stacy watching us from the other side of the dance floor. She looked really annoyed. But I didn't let that bother me. After all, she may have had the leading role in the play, but I was the one dancing with the leading man — and I had stolen the show!

Don't Miss
GIRL TALK #9
PEER PRESSURE

I looked toward the front of the auditorium at Mr. Hansen, the principal of Bradley Junior High. "Today I will announce the names of the Bradley Junior High Winter Carnival Olympic team," he said.

Mr. Hansen began to read the team lists and I started worrying about my tryouts again.

"Now we come to a new event, synchronized skating. The two pairs will be Stacy Hansen with Kim Kushner and Katie Campbell. . ."

For a second, I was sure that I was going to float right out of my seat and up to the ceiling. I had made it!

I met up with my friends after the assembly.

"Hey, guys! What's wrong?" I asked, looking at their solemn expressions.

"I'm sorry," Sabrina blurted out.

"Sorry?" I asked, totally confused. "What are you talking about?"

"You didn't hear?" Sabrina gasped. "Katie, Mr. Hansen said your partner is . . . Laurel Spencer."

Laurel Spencer! My jaw dropped open. There had to be a mistake!

LOOK FOR THESE OTHER AWESOME
GIRL TALK BOOKS!

MORE GIRL TALK TITLES TO LOOK FOR

Nonfiction

ASK ALLIE 101 answers to your questions about boys, friends, family, and school!

YOUR PERSONALITY QUIZ Fun, easy quizzes to help you discover the real you!

BOYTALK: HOW TO TALK TO YOUR FAVORITE GUY